LIGHT

OF

KASABAN

THOMAS HOWARD RILEY

To Allison. To Evan. To Hannah. And to my Mom and Dad.
With special thanks to Rowena.

THE

LIGHT

OF

KASABAN

A book is never *just* a story.
It is a collaboration between the author and your imagination.
So every book is a different book depending on who reads it.
A book changes every time it changes hands.
That is truly extraordinary.

CONTENTS

1

Execution Day

THE FIRST OF EVERY MONTH was execution day. Saya forced her feet to stand there, forced her eyes to see, making herself one more anonymous face among the broiling crowd in the forum, watching people like her being cast into the flames.

It had been so for as long as she could remember. Whenever she closed her eyes she became a child again, clutching at her mother's robes, one little hand a claw around the only two of her mother's fingers that would fit in her tiny palm.

Now she stood taller than her mother had. Now she came alone to watch the smoke rising above the pale simmering rooftops, a brutal sun presiding over the screams. Her hand closed around the shard of stone in her pocket, squeezing and releasing until her fingers bled.

I must bear witness. I owe them that much.

She wore a crown of sweat, every other breath sending a drop plummeting down her forehead, behind her ears, or the back of her neck. Soon enough it would run like rain, her robes wicking it from her until they became a second skin. She hated standing out in the open in the noontide of a Kasaban sun, but she would not leave until it was done. Each of them deserved at least one witness who was of their own kind.

Like me.

They were all just people like her—magi, the ones blessed to touch the infinite source, gifted to draw forth streams of magick and bind them together to create wonders in the world.

Men and women and little children.

The unlucky ones. The ones who were caught.

The Priests would make exemptions for some of the captured—the men and the boys. Some anyway, the ones they judged redeemable. The women and girls were never spared. Even the little babies were taken to the fires and burned alive for what they were.

Someone like me.

This was her world, where merely to exist was itself a criminal act.

A woman who could use magick was an abomination, they said. A loathsome creature vomited up from the depths of the deepest hell. These were the words Saya heard every day of her life, from the mouths of normals, laughing in cafes as though they were musing about their favorite clouds, not the agony of real people.

The elders said it had not always been so. This had once been the city of Kasaban, the jewel of the white desert, full of history and treasures of ages past.

But that all changed the day the Priests came.

Their armies had swept over Kasaban as they marched onward to fulfill the religious urge for conquest inherited from their one and only god, seeking to spread the law of their Lord of Truth and his bottomless appetite for suffering to every corner of the world.

The once-peaceful city of Saya's cherished memories had become the front line of a holy crusade, conquered and occupied by the Ministry. It was their law that now governed her life.

A gap opened in the crowd just then, forced wide by soldiers with heavy spears, a path leading from the Incarnation Temple, across the Invocation Square to the wide elevated stone platform at its center.

It is time.

That gap in the crowd meant death. It meant the condemned were approaching. Saya closed her eyes and tried to wish it closed, grinding her teeth, knuckles white. She tried to wake up from the nightmare. But when she opened her eyes, the white stone walls of her city were still there, a blinding sun crushing her beneath a mountain of light.

She watched as the condemned were prodded toward the stone platform—three men and five women. Bare feet turned chalk white from desert dust. Robes turned to rags, stained from sweat, soaked and dried a dozen times, forming rings in many layers across their chests and under their arms.

They reached out to the crowd on either side, but no one even dared hold out a comforting hand. At the center of a thousand people, but all alone.

Their eyes went everywhere, mouths frozen, terrified and confused, minds swimming in a sea of tinwood leaf tea, just enough of a dose to keep them from concentrating well enough to use their magick. But not so much that they wouldn't feel every instant of pain.

Saya whispered apologies to each of them as they passed her. *I'm sorry. I don't know what to do. I'm so sorry. I've tried to wake us up from this dream, but I can't.*

Soldiers wearing black metal armor beneath white robes beat and kicked them onward. When one of the men stumbled on numb legs, they thrashed him until he was back in line.

One woman sobbed, too desiccated to produce tears. Saya was drawn to her. Young, like she was. Black of hair, like she was. Skin darker than her mother's but lighter than her father's, just like she had. This young woman was her. She was looking at herself, another Saya Ani Anai, ushered toward the flames.

Saya couldn't bear to look her in the eyes as she stumbled, bare feet caked in white, face bruised, lip split, hair a mottled mess of straw bedding and the spit of her captor guards. She hobbled as if her ribs had been broken. They likely had been.

The people of her city did not cheer. The sun kept them quiet. Saya could never tell how many of them wept inside like she did, and how many bit their lips in anticipation for what was to come.

The soldiers forced the condemned up polished steps to the wide stone platform, white as Kasaban sand. There they were separated and precisely arranged for the burning.

The Priests of the Ministry and their acolytes gathered behind them, adorned in pure white robes, hooded, faces hidden beneath expressionless alabaster masks painted in austere gold, perfectly round holes for the eyes and mouth. The masks looked like they were always staring, always screaming. Saya was terrified of them.

The Priests never touched the condemned, stepping around them as one might a pile of rotten dung. The golden masks screamed in silence at them, guiding them with sticks wrapped tightly in hide, poking and swatting at them like pack mules.

Even when killing us they allow us no dignity.

She felt tears in her eyes and rage in her fists, but there was nowhere for it to go. She could not scream. She could not weep. She could not claw at the guards or pummel the Priests with her fists. If she stood out from the crowd they would know what she was. They would chase her. They would catch her. They would kill her. Then the children she protected would have no one.

She forced her fingers apart. She tilted her head back until the tears were swallowed up by her eyes. She looked at the pale blue Kasaban sky, an ocean above her, not a cloud in sight. It was an infinite vault where she could put all her emotions. She had so many. She could not hold them. If she tried they would crush her. She would never move again.

She felt a featherlight finger slide across the skin of her arm. Her heart turned upside down and she nearly gasped, but she caught the sound in her throat and forced it down with a gulp.

That was how Radir always alerted her to his presence. Even at home when there was no need to pretend they did not know each other, the boy would still give her a fright. He had lived through sixteen summers, and none of them had softened his joy at making her jump. But at home it was a game. Here it was a necessity. If one of them happened to be tracked, it would do no good to set the Priests on the other's trail.

"What are you doing here?" she whispered.

"Is this where you are always disappearing to, Saya Ani Anai?" he asked. He was the only one who called her by her given name. The other children always called her Sayani.

"No," she hissed. "You are stupid to come here. Go home now."

They stood side by side, eyes ahead, never once glancing at each other. He had chosen his favorite pale red robe, like the terra-cotta shingles atop the Moneychanger's compound across from the old waterworks.

"You know what they do here?" His voice turned severe. It sounded foreign on his tongue.

"Yes. You ask as if I have not lived here my whole life."

He did not respond for a long time, watching each of the condemned ceremonially bound at their wrists and ankles. "Why do you watch?" he finally asked.

She thought she might cry. She was surprised when she didn't. "So that I never forget why we must be vigilant, why we must work so hard to cover our tracks. I do it so that I never feel that it is permissible to be lazy even just the once, to skip a step here, a precaution there. I must always remember what will happen to us if we aren't careful."

Saying it aloud felt good. It made her feel strong. It reminded her that even in this terrible place there were things she could control. There had to be. It was the only way she could hold on.

"You shouldn't have to do this alone, Saya," Radir said.

"I used to come with Khersas."

"Khersas is dead."

"No." If only her will could make it so.

"Khersas is dead, Saya."

"He's not dead. He's not gone. He's still here. He's still real. He's still alive in my heart."

"Okay," he said.

"I'm sorry."

He brushed it off. "None of the little ones have ever seen it, have they?"

She almost turned to look at him. She needed to see his narrow eyes and that familiar little smirk he called a smile. She needed something of *home* so badly in that moment. "No. We...I...found them all before they were old enough to have known. I pray they never need to. I pray this will all end before they are old enough to need to know." She paused. "I wish I had found you sooner, too."

"So that is why you never allow any of them to leave home on the first of the moons." His hood jiggled in the corner of her eye as he nodded agreement. "When the warren-boss and his gang beat my neighbor all the way to death and left him in a puddle of blood, I thought it was the worst thing I would ever see. I said as much. Out loud. The very next day I saw what they do here. I don't say such things out loud anymore."

"It can't be like this always," Saya said. She did not know if it was true, only that it *had* to be true. It had to or there was no way to make her feet take another step.

"Since before we were born. Your parents knew better days perhaps."

Saya said nothing. *My parents.* The fear and shame punched her insides so hard she shuddered. She looked up and away. Seeing the agony of horrible death was better than the memories.

The Priests prepared a massive fire pit behind the row of condemned. Their acolytes set logs atop a deep pile of dried desert scrub. Then they set it alight. It crackled. It popped. It roared to life, tongues of flame licking the air.

Iron basins, each as wide as a cooking kettle, were brought forth and set into polished tripod ring stands, one before each of the condemned. A Priest with a golden ladle walked to each basin, a young acolyte struggling with a heavy bucket behind him. The ladle dipped into the bucket three times for each of the basins. Each time it poured twisted slivers of metal into them.

The metal that burns. And it burned hot. White hot. And its flame could outshine the sun. Water could not dowse it, only make it worse.

The first man was made to kneel before his basin. Even full of tinwood leaf tea, he understood what was happening. He struggled uselessly against the soldiers, fingers clawing at their white cloaks, heels kicking at the black metal of the armor underneath. His eyes were frantic, his limbs weak, uncoordinated from the sedative, shivering despite the relentless heat.

The others watched him flail and they all became hopeless, wailing a hideous dissonant dirge. The Priests stood back all the while, golden terror masks screaming silently, white robes pure and untouched, letting their soldiers do the base work of touching the unclean.

All three of the men were set to kneel. A Priest lined up behind each man, holding long poles with semicircular hooks at one end, like crescent moons, and placed one around the back of each neck. The men went still. There was nothing else now between them and what was to come, not even time.

The Priests pushed hard on the first crescent pole. The man struggled against it, straining every sinew in his back to push away. It was useless. They forced his face into the basin, and then the metal shavings were lit with a ceremonial flint. They burst instantly into white-hot flame.

The metal that burns.

Khersas had once described to her what the heat did to them—the skin bubbling and melting, the eyes bursting in hissing gouts of steam, the tongues roasting in their mouths. He had gone on to feel it for himself not long after.

Saya began to cry.

The women lasted the longest. This was intentional. They were strapped to poles or tables above the fires, the flames beginning at their feet. At least they started with the head for the men, killing them quickly. For the women it was always much worse. Different punishments for the same crime, decided based on the degree to which the Priests hated the ones committing them.

The sounds they made were inhuman. They always were. Long grotesque reptilian whines, hopeless scratchy animal wails. Hair burned away. Skin blackened. One by one they went quiet. It seemed to take centuries.

Saya wiped fiercely at her eyes, furious that the Priests had made her betray her sorrow. She dried them as best she could, but they flowed again at every new scream.

Radir noticed. "Don't cry, Saya. No matter how bad today is, there is always a chance that tomorrow will be better, and..." He trailed off.

"...and the good thing about tomorrows is that there always is one." She smiled until tears coated her lips.

She forced herself to look, no matter how strong the tears came on. She had to see. She had to remember. The smoke slid into her nose no matter how hard she tried to hold her breath against it, sickly sweet, the bleak story of her people told through the scent of their flesh roasting.

When the last of the screams finally subsided, the acolytes dragged the bodies back to the fire pits and kicked them in, trusting the ordinary flames to consume them, rendering them into ash and bone.

"I wish I could fight them," Radir said. "I wish I could stop this. I wish I was strong enough."

"Someday we will be," she said. "We shall not be weak forever. Leave now, come back stronger, and we will fight again when we can win."

He nodded. He said nothing more after that.

Once the fires were quenched, the normal thieves and murderers were brought forward and either hanged unceremoniously at the gallows or beheaded. It seemed so horrifically mundane after what the fire had done to its victims.

"I heard from an ice den thief that the Priests might be bringing Glassdogs to Kasaban," Radir said.

Saya shuddered. "Have you ever seen one?"

He shook his head. "Like Glasseyes, they say. Only worse. They never take the lenses off their eyes."

"They go mad, Khersas told me. Men never allowed to see the real world, forced to only look at magick. They become animals, hounds to sniff out afterglow. He said he had seen the Priests use them when they pacified Madinas." She paused. "This is very bad. It will make it that much harder for us to move freely."

"And with the money already low this month," he said.

She closed her eyes and sighed. "I know."

"I will warn the children. I thought you should know."

"Thank you."

Every day they take a little more of what we are. Every day they make it harder for me to keep us from ending up on that stage.

The Priests had changed the language of this place to their common Westrin tongue, and had punished those who dared yet teach the desert tongue of old. Saya had never learned the words her ancestors once used. Even that little piece of the past had been stolen from her.

They had shuttered the temples and extinguished the gods of every pantheon, replacing them with altars of devotion to their Lord of Truth. They had slaughtered the hallowed templars and crushed revolts of the faithful.

Our gods were murdered.

The Ministry was ruthless and efficient. Tureg, Maglene, Gehevra, and Luerdiccas—every god and goddess cast down. One by one, they killed them all.

All save one.

They left standing the temples of Holy Juna. Hers alone. Because she was the goddess of peace and patience and kindness, who encouraged piety and obedience to community—all of which were close enough to *subservience* in the eyes of the Priests. That was what they wanted most, after all.

The elders used to tell stories of the War of Centuries, of how Holy Juna saved the people by turning herself into a light so bright she outshined the sun, leaving no shadows and turning her enemies to dust. But the Priests had changed the stone carvings to say it was their Lord of Truth who shined the light, and Holy Juna was only there to kneel before him in worship.

Even the scraps of our heritage the Priests leave behind for us are corrupted beyond salvaging.

And then they turned her people against her, against all those like her. The sacred elders of magick were murdered, and the people they once taught to bring beauty and joy into this world with their sacred gifts were declared fugitive—banned, exiled, hunted.

All that remained were the newly born. And the Priests worked methodically to ensure their extermination. So many informants had been cultivated that Saya could trust almost no one.

And, of course, the fires burned every month so that those like her could always see and smell and hear the fate that awaited them if they slipped up for but one moment.

"Leave in a different direction than me," she said. "We must not be seen together."

She did not see Radir nod, but she knew he had. He always did when she asked something of him. He turned and vanished into the crowd. She wanted to watch him go, poor, sweet Radir, but she dared not. Even a little-too-long glance could be divined by Priests and their informants as a connection.

I will see you at home.

She turned and walked away, swallowing a lump of sorrow the size of a riverstone, leaving behind the ashes of those lost souls who would never have a chance to be free.

She threaded a path through the carts of anemic fish from the pond, already warm in the shade of the cart awnings, and then those of the well-connected fishermen who were permitted access to the river. She drifted between red and white striped sandmerchants from Rhodas, and even a Besembrian lamb-monger haggling with a pair of wealthy chain-breakers out of Nabena, gold bracelets with dangling chains where they had once worn irons.

Even here she could never quite shake the feeling of someone following her. She saw far too many wrists wearing the Holy Annunkebar pendant of the Priests, a circle of orange flames about a white center worn on a black band, the symbol of one who has been rewarded for turning in one of her kind to be sent to the fires.

But she considered it a good thing. It meant she never let her guard down. Not even for a moment.

That left little time to think of everything else it took to survive in this place. Like where would the money come from? Would they have enough food? Enough medicine? Enough extra to afford the bribe to keep their home a secret? Had any of the others been caught? Would she return home to find one of the children gone, never to be seen again?

The crowds always thickened when she reached the Flowergarden around the aqueduct square beside the Rhoda Gate. She joined the masses and rejoiced, melding into the multitude of faces, disappearing.

She stifled her rage as she stepped past a Priest in his white robes and hideous gold mask. She was afraid that she might not be able to prevent herself from touching the source out of reflex.

The Priests were all users of magick. One had to be to gain even that low rank within their Ministry. And like all magi, if they were close enough they could sense magick being rendered before it became real, even sense someone touching the source just for an instant.

She could have rendered magick, created a bubble of bending light around herself, becoming nearly invisible. But she didn't. Because being invisible in Kasaban was not so easy. For even if she could disappear from the naked eye, the afterglow of her magick couldn't hide from the hunters. Not with Glasseyes always peering through their crystal lenses for every stain of magick they could find, using it to track her back to even the best of her hidden places.

She had witnessed less-than-careful children taken right off the street to be burned for such things. Saya would not allow them to take her that way—to sedate her and condemn her. She would hide or she would die, she had always promised herself. She would never be captured.

She would die one day, but by her own choosing; not theirs. She already knew the place and time where her life would end—whenever the children of her school needed her to. That would be the day she would leave this world, and not before. Nothing else but the end of her life would keep her from protecting them.

She cherished her invisibility, embraced it as her ethos. Hidden self, hidden home. She even learned from Khersas how to do it without magick, how to blend into the masses on the busiest thoroughfares, dissolving into the press of bodies, one more anonymous face amid the throng. Anonymity was her armor, a refuge more impregnable than the strongest mountain citadel.

Hiding to survive was better than fighting every moment of every day to live. Invisibility was better than armor. No one could fight the Priests. She had seen foolish people try.

Fighting by itself wasn't brave. Protecting someone was brave. And sometimes the best way to protect what was most precious was to run, to hide, to survive.

She withdrew the shard of white stone from her pocket, held so tightly for so many years its surface had been smoothed halfway to a fine polish, decorated with her fingerprints in blood. A piece of the old roof where her parents had raised her, broken loose when the Priests came to smash through the wall and take them away, the only thing Saya's tiny hand had managed to grab hold of before she had to run away forever.

Fighting and dying means nothing if it damns the ones who depend on you.

She would tell her parents that if they hadn't already found out for themselves so many years ago. Leaving her all alone. To grow up in this place. Having to carve a niche for herself in this hell. She would never put anyone else through that.

Leave now. Come back stronger. Fight when you can win.

She looked at the sun, high in the sky.

The light of Kasaban burns all it touches, love, hope, joy. Nothing can withstand it. The heat bakes flesh and stone. The winds whisper like flames. The sun does not forgive.

She had to get back. The children would begin to worry.

2

Sevastin Karda

SEVASTIN KARDA WAS CLEANING white sand from under his fingernails with a bloody iron needle when they brought him the infant.

He set down the needle and looked at the cooing baby they carried, swaddled in old ivory rags. Both of his subordinates still wore the gilded facemasks and white robes of crusade, as he did, open eyes and open mouth, screaming at the souls of the unholy.

He spun the needle on his desk. Its sharp end came to rest on the infant. He could see over the swaddling that the skin was the savaged brown of the southern deserts.

"Why have you brought me this thing?" he asked.

"Found within a home we raided," Seppel said.

"Mother and father both touched by light," Faral nodded.

"Touched by light, but not sanctified by the Holy Ministry."

"No, Prelate Karda," Seppel said. "Both were rogues, using magick all their lives without our guidance."

Karda yawned. "Burn the mother in the fire, of course."

"Of course, Prelate Karda. Burn the mother, yes."

"From the bottom up," Karda reminded them. Some of his Priests had grown weak of stomach after hearing the screams of these filthy demons as they burned.

"Yes, Prelate Karda."

Kasaban was the front line of the holy crusade. Here they were surrounded by demons dressed as men and women, who could twist the glorious white light of the Lord of Truth into profane rogue magick. It was Karda's duty to stop them, and all his superiors within the Ministry were watching closely.

"Age of the father?" Sevastin Karda asked.

"Thirty-eight summers, Prelate Karda."

He nodded severely. *If only we had found him sooner.* "Too old for automatic indoctrination into our rolls then. He must also burn. Did the father repent?"

"Yes. After questioning, Prelate Karda."

"Burn him by the head then."

"Yes, Prelate Karda."

Karda retrieved the needle once more. But the two of them remained, holding the child. "What is it?"

"The infant, Prelate Karda," Faral said. "Our Glasseyes discovered a glow from the infant."

"It has exhibited magick ability?"

"Yes, Prelate Karda. We have never seen anything like it. Touching the source so young. This child is truly extraordinary."

"Is the infant male or female?" Sevastin Karda asked.

Seppel paused. "Female, Prelate Karda."

"Hmmm," Karda said. "Burn it as well."

His subordinates exchanged a glance.

Karda rolled his eyes. "What?"

"Brother Purdikkas was asking," Faral said. "Well, he was asking if we might burn this one from the head as well, with fire-metal in the burning bowl. So the death might be more... instantaneous."

Sevastin Karda set down the needle once more. He clasped his hands together about one knee, fingers interlocking. "Brother Purdikkas wants to burn the infant in such a way that it feels no pain."

"Yes, Prelate Karda."

"This infant is a woman with magick ability. This thing in your arms is a demon, an abomination. It must burn. Women are not permitted to touch the source of magick, lest they taint the white light of possibility, the domain of our Lord of Truth, who is also the Lord of Magick, granted to us to keep pure and clean until his return."

"Yes, Prelate Karda," they both said at once.

Sevastin Karda cracked a half-smile. "Tell Brother Purdikkas to burn the infant from the feet, horizontally, to maximize its agony to equal its rarity."

He could not see either of their faces beneath the masks, but he knew his words made them uneasy. Yet when the fate of the world was at stake, one had to become used to feeling uneasy.

"Oh, and Brothers?"

"Yes, Prelate Karda?"

"Tell him to burn the infant first. Make the mother watch. I want her soul to understand the terrible crime she committed by giving birth to it."

They nodded and exited the room.

Sevastin Karda returned to cleaning the white desert dust from under his fingernails with the bloody iron nail.

3

Poor Girl

SAYA ANI ANAI WAS a poor girl and everyone knew it.

Her robes were plain ivory, salt-stained and thinned by age, the end of one sleeve frayed, the lower fringes pulling a train of loose threads along the ground behind her. If they could have seen the state of her sandals they would have laughed.

Every breath coated her nose in dust until she could smell little else. The scent lived within her. Only fresh sun sweat and roasting garlic from the meat friers were able to cut through it.

Her feet were white as clouds, stained well past her ankles from a lifetime of walking the outermost edges of every street, where the sweepers piled high the hot white sand and dust of Kasaban.

The pristine clear middle of every street was not meant for poor girls like Saya. Any who refused to cede the middle to the wealthy would find their skulls on the receiving end of a truncheon the first time one of the city governor's street soldiers noticed them.

The dunemakers were out in force early this morning after the past night's heavy winds, their heavy push-brooms raising mountain ranges of fine salty sand and chalky powder, driving them up against the walls in an endless tectonic ballet, belching pale plumes into the air with every sweep. They shuffled along, shunting the white desert sand and dust out of the middle of the streets, clearing way for the feet of the rich. Dumping it all in the path of the poor instead.

So she trudged through coarse ankle-high powder as she did every morning, her arm brushing the white walls of houses and shops, wearing away at the fabric of her robe until her shoulder could be seen through it.

But Saya did not mind it. Walking on the edge offered a wide view of all the people moving up and down the avenues. Especially the little children darting to and fro like sparrows— laughing, chasing, playing, even thieving if they were short enough not to be noticed.

They were so full of life. Saya envied them. She could barely remember what it had been like to be that carefree, back when her father's arms had been the safest place in the world, and her mother had been the only god she had ever needed.

Her eyes narrowed on two little ones in particular, each no more than three or four years of age, one with black hair, the other brown, wearing matching little trousers and shirts of blue and green. They plodded along like a pair of little ducklings in the wake of a district overseer in a plumed cap. The man had a smile as wide as he was corrupt, a coinpurse fat with bribes slapping against his hip with every step.

She assumed he must have been their father until she saw one of them wave his tiny little hand in the air. The coinpurse tore open as if a silent, razor-sharp knife had cut it, just enough for the silver coins to dribble out in a sparkling stream. They never reached the ground. The other child made two fists, and the coins slowed and came to rest in the air at his knees, hovering like glistening hummingbirds.

Saya's eyes widened. They were two little cutpurses...who wielded magick to do the cutting. The children snatched the coins greedily out of the air, stuffing them in their pockets. No one else had seen the children at their work, but one last coin must have been caught in the hole, finally jostled out by the man's steps.

Saya watched it tumble out. Her heart froze in her chest. She thought of the fires.

The coin hit the ground with a terrifying little ping, bounced twice, then rattled to a stop. The man turned and stared at them, lip curling into a snarl. The children froze under his gaze. It would take only a quick shout to summon a street soldier or a Priest in a gold mask to drag them away to burn.

Saya forgot how to speak. She forgot how to walk. Her breath felt like steam. Sweat poured down the sides of her face. Her arms and legs were on fire, numb but burning. Her feet grew roots into the earth, holding her there. She squeezed the sharp edges of the stone in her pocket until her fingers bled.

If he realizes what they have done, they die.

She closed her eyes. Opened them. Sucked in a breath.

Do something!

Her legs surged into motion. She flowed up to the man, wearing a smile. His eyes leapt to her, tore her apart. Outside she wore a flirtatious smile. Inside she screamed.

She felt fear crawl all across her. His eyes were every bead of sweat sliding down her body, every droplet that plummeted from her chin. His stare burned like the sun on her skin.

She summoned every bit of strength to keep from withering before his stare. "Pardon me," she said. "I dropped my coin. Would you help me?" Her throat closed up. Her ears felt thick and distant. She was not sure how she managed to get the words out without vomiting. She prayed to Holy Juna that she could remain on her feet long enough to convince him.

Shine your light for me, Holy Juna. Please.

She dipped her mind into the pure liquid possibility of the source, and felt her familiar streams of magick swimming to her, ready to bind together, ready to make her and these two children invisible if she had to. But she held back.

He had not called them out as thieves yet, but he seemed skeptical.

Saya puffed out her lower lip and tried to look helpless, hoping he would see her wide eyes and soft skin and welcoming smile rather than the old robes hanging on her shoulders. If he noticed, he would realize that someone like her would never have a silver to her name.

Please.

The man's expression softened. He crouched down and plucked the coin off the ground, casually handing her his own money. She thanked him profusely, muttering apologies for her two children, politely declining when he asked if he could father two more for her. He smiled at his own foul joke, turned, and walked away.

Saya tried to keep her face calm while she remembered how to breathe. At last her throat opened and she gulped a mouthful of sunshine and chalky dust. She coughed and spat until she felt herself again.

She then turned her gaze to the two tiny thieves. She held the silver between thumb and forefinger.

They stared at it, shaking.

"You must be more careful," she said.

They nodded, mouths agape.

"I can take you somewhere," she said. "Somewhere safe for people like us, where you can learn to be careful."

They looked at each other, then back at her.

"I can take you to my school. It is a place for children who are special, like you. A home for little ones who have no one else to protect them. You will be welcome there if you wish. Two special boys like you will fit right in."

They agreed to follow her, though they did so cautiously, not yet trusting her. They were wise in that, she thought. Trusting someone too quickly in Kasaban was the surest way to die.

She turned down an alley and led them through an abandoned metalworker's shop, into another alley, and through a narrow space between two hostelries. She lifted a shuttered window and dropped down into a basement, through a passageway and up into an empty house, then out through a side door, hidden from the outside by overgrown vines.

Here she had a stone washbasin and a sealed jar of water waiting. "Every time you bind the streams of magick, you leave a stain in the air, and on yourselves. The stains glow to the hunters. The Priests have ways to see the stains you leave and follow you, even if you cannot see them. You must learn to hide these."

She poured water into the basin and made them dip their hands in water and splash it on themselves, soaking their clothes as much as possible.

"Water quickens the decay of the invisible stains of magick," she told them. She made them both scrub their hands with Ranum crystal soaps and obsidian sand. She did the same.

"I'm not dirty," the smaller boy complained.

"You rendered magick," she said. "You used your fingers to help your mind tell your magick where to go. Even making just that little bit will coat your fingertips with afterglow, and make a little cloud of it in the air where you did it. Invisible to you and to me, but not to a Glasseye's crystal lens. It will cling to your hands, and anything you touch. Like the coins. You must wash them also."

She waited while they did.

There would be tiny clouds of afterglow left behind in the street as well, and on the man's coinpurse, but small enough for a bright sun to wash out. She hoped.

"The Glasseyes hunt magi like us for the Priests. With the lenses they carry, they can see such invisible things as plain as day, and follow little boys and girls like a trail of breadcrumbs. Once they have seen the stains of magick you leave behind it is next to impossible to escape the hunters. If they find your afterglow, they can record its shape, and teach their people how to block it. If one of their Stoppers knows the feel of your magick, they can cut you off from your power merely by standing close to you. Do you understand now why you need to be more careful?"

They both nodded mutely.

She always washed herself after she rendered magick. Always, before even thinking about returning home. All her students were required to do the same. It was painstaking, dull, and repetitive. But there was a reason why it had to be done.

This was the reason she forced herself to watch every excruciation the Priests performed. So that every time she thought of skipping a step during cleaning, or of not paying attention to what she touched along the way, she would remember the screams of the dying as they burned.

She led the boys down a narrow path behind a row of houses, and through many turns until she arrived at a storm drain. She could have taken a straighter path to it, but the winding nature of the journey was designed to throw off a hunter.

She lifted the cover—wooden planks overgrown with thick moss—revealing a narrow chute. The last rain had been sixty days hence. It was dry as bleached bones in the harsh Kasaban sun.

She slid down it, beckoning them to follow. It was a shallow decline, but as dry as it was, they were forced to wriggle most of the way. The two boys looked around, mystified. Saya tugged on a string to pull the planks back into place over the hole.

It was dark here, and quickly grew darker as she went further from the chute. This was the entrance to the ancient brick sewers that crawled beneath the streets of Kasaban. She lit no torch, for she knew well the way, and just as it became as dark as night, it began to brighten again with a new source of light ahead.

She led them down a tunnel, and up a flight of stone steps, until at last she reached a blank wall where the stairs dead-ended. She looked up into the light of morning above, shining down on her through the criss-crossed iron bars of another storm grate. She tugged at the corner where a rope ladder was hidden. She pulled it taut, and began to climb. When she reached the top, she tapped thrice on the iron grate, waited, then thrice more. She waited, swaying gently on the ladder.

A shadow appeared atop the grate, hands clasped the iron bars, and the metal squeaked and groaned as it was lifted off from above. Saya pulled herself up and out, then peeked her head back down, flashing a comforting smile. She motioned them to climb up after her, and waited patiently for them both.

Whichever of her students had removed the grate was gone. It must have been Noqer. He was the only one strong enough to lift it by himself other than Radir, and Radir would have waited for her.

The space was forty paces long and wide, a two-story house leaning against one wall, and a small half-collapsed outbuilding overgrown with trees on the adjacent one. Ash and cedar sprung up around the perimeter, lining four identical fifteen-foot-high red brick walls surrounding the compound. An abundant orange tree possessed one corner. In the other lived a drooping willow, its roots long since grown into the irrigation drain tunnels to drink.

The boys stared wide-eyed all around.

Saya understood why. This place was a secret only she and her students knew about, a hidden grotto deep within a bustling city.

What had once been an entrance to this courtyard had been bricked over to match the walls and the two-story shops lining the alleys outside, four high walls of red stone and mortar that no one paid any attention to. Saya glanced over at the ruined house, the outbuilding that was now missing two walls, a sacrifice well worth the privacy.

The outer walls around this courtyard were now seamless. From the outside, one could walk in the narrow alleys all the way around it and only see the four high brick walls. It was just something to walk past, like any of the other walled compounds of the wealthy warren-bosses. A safe place, where never again would anyone be able to stumble upon her and take her by surprise the way they had her little brother, where she would never be tempted to make the choice to fight back like her mother and father had.

The only entrance now was underground, through the drain. She heaved the grate back into place. It clanged into its grooves, and she covered it with canvas and a pile of leaves.

"This is home," she said. "This is the School."

Saya led them to the main house, two stories high and full of small rooms, repurposed as bedrooms. She stepped up to the porch beside the old bench, pulled open a dark door, and led them inside a small workshop lit by candles. A row of boots and sandals of every size and variety and state of disrepair lined one wall. On the other wall leaned two fishing rods, stacks of firewood, twine, metal cups, and cloaks hung from hooks above them. It smelled of dirt and wood and home.

She led them to the end of the hall and into the homeroom. It was the largest, the only one that could comfortably accommodate all her students. It was already occupied—full, in fact—with each of the scratched and faded couches stuffed with children playing their favorite guessing games.

Saya stopped in the doorway, greeted with silence and stares. She brought forth her two little newcomers, leading each of them by the hand. She smiled, and the silence was broken.

"Sayani! Sayani! You're back!" Lili was always the first to come forward. She scampered across the room, clapping her hands wildly in celebration, locks of sunset-brown hair hopping about her shoulders. At six summers, she was nearest to the age of the two boys, and she rushed to them, a host of little questions flapping from her mouth before Saya could protest.

"Hush," Mara suggested. "You'll frighten them." Mara revered obedience, and wanted everyone to be sure they were aware of her opinion on the matter. She demanded it even of her hair, maintaining a length of bangs to her brow, and a length of the rest to just below her ears, ruthlessly enforced by a pair of shears she always kept in her pocket.

Lili sneered a little sneer at Mara. "New boys," she said, as if it was a proper excuse.

Mara, twice Lili's age, rolled her eyes but smiled and took each boy by the hands and bowed, eyes closed, drawing the backs of their hands up to her forehead in the old way that a servant of Holy Juna greeted a stranger. "Welcome," she said.

"Yes, welcome," Noqer said, trying to make his fourteen-year-old voice husky, but failing in startling fashion. "Welcome to two more mouths to feed." He folded his arms across his chest and puffed himself up, annoyed, his dark eyes looking askance.

"There will be none of that talk," Saya said. "We welcome everyone who is like us." Though even she had to admit a weight in her belly at the thought of extra food they might need this month and the next.

"Yes," Adrani agreed, throwing her long black braid over one shoulder. Her eyes were a luscious green, and her skin pure copper and as smooth as polished stone, nary a blemish upon her anywhere. "You are just grumpy because you couldn't manage to catch as many fish out at the pond today as I did." She giggled and winked at him.

Although she was only a year younger than he, Noqer dismissed her as if she were a baby. "If I could have used my *skill* at the pond, we would have more fish than we could ever eat."

The temperature in the room grew noticeably warmer very suddenly.

"Stop it, Radir," Noqer said. "I'm already sweating and I just washed my shirts."

"We can't use our powers outside the school and you know it," Lili said, turning her chin up authoritatively. "Sayani says so."

Noqer grumbled.

"I will stop when you pipe down," Radir said, standing alone behind one of the couches, a shimmer of sparkling color steaming off his skin. He liked to make the temperature flare to get someone's attention. In a place like Kasaban, heat was social currency.

Saya nodded to him.

He smiled and the heat dissipated.

"We have guests," Saya said. "I expect the proper manners from each of you." She was particularly worried about Noqer. He had thrown a fit when Tana first came to the school.

Saya knelt before the boys, a hand on each of their shoulders. "My name is Saya Ani Anai," she said. "My students call me Sayani."

"Sayani means *my light*," Lili explained. "Her given name means..." She tapped her chin, suddenly perturbed. "I don't know what."

"What are *their* names?" Serine asked, staring with wide eyes.

"I do not yet know," Saya said. She looked down at them both. "Would you like to introduce yourselves to my other students?"

The two boys responded by trying to hide in her robes.

"Why don't all of you go first," Saya said, with a wave of her arm. "Left to right. We will start with you, Sotta."

Sotta blinked in surprise as if he had not been aware that he was seated leftmost. He shifted uncomfortably, and the old wood of the couch frame creaked under his weight. His wide nose twitched. He was by far the roundest little boy Saya had ever seen. When she first brought him here, he had made her promise to love him *more than his circumference*, because, he said, *that would be a lot.*

"I am Sotta," Sotta said. "I have seen ten summers."

Aafi went next. He was perpetually skin and bones. Adrani always teased him that if he wasn't careful he would end up folded between the pages of one of Saya's books. "I am Aafi, and I am nine summers old."

"And you have eaten ten summers worth of food," said Sotta beside him. He laughed and elbowed Aafi playfully.

"You never finish your meals anyway," Aafi accused. "I prevent you from being wasteful."

"Between the two of you, it evens out," said Adrani. "I am Adrani, and I am thirteen summers old." She smiled substantially.

"I am Qudra," said the first boy on the next couch. "I am eight summers old, including the one we are in now." He said nothing more. Knowing him, Saya presumed he was preoccupied thinking up the next mischief he would get up to.

"I am Tana," said the little flaxen-haired girl beside him. "And I am also eight summers old, but I am older than Qudra because he was born in the spring and I was born the autumn before."

"Yes, we all know how smart you are," said Tashim beside her. "You mention it all the time."

Tana frowned at him, and crossed her arms, pouting.

"I am Tashim," the boy said. "And I am eleven summers *and* winters old." He loved pointing that out, not so much because it made him seem older, but rather because he obsessed over everyone understanding the precise number of everything, even the seasons of his life. Especially the number of birthmarks scribbling a constellation across one cheek and half his forehead.

The little girl who sat on the other side of him mimicked his every gesture and expression, frequently glancing over at him to make sure she was doing it properly. "I am Serine, and I have seen seven summers." She was Tashim's shadow, they were always practicing together.

"Two peas in a pod," said Noqer, rolling his eyes at them, still annoyed. "I am Noqer. I am fourteen summers old." He said it as if it was a compulsory duty that he despised.

"I am Radir." He wore his finest borrowed crimson robe, smiling both darkly and sweetly, the mole on his left cheek making him adorable to her no matter how much he tried to be made of stone. "I have lived sixteen summers."

Radir kept to himself much of the time, but he was patient, and he always looked after the children when she needed him to. Saya was grateful for him every day.

The next boy was too shy to speak, forcing Saya to introduce him herself. "That is Faloush. He is nine summers old, aren't you?"

Faloush nodded. He had drawn a little black mustache on his upper lip with charcoal, and Saya had a difficult time not bursting into laughter at the sight of it.

"I am Raba," the next boy quickly said, before she could speak for him. He said the words so abruptly that a burst of spittle flew out of his mouth along with them. The others laughed, and his round cheeks reddened visibly. "I am eight summers old."

"I am Mara," Mara said, shaking the little newcomers' hands as if they were visiting dignitaries from a foreign king. "I am twelve summers old."

"And that leaves me," said Lili, clapping cheerfully all over again. "I am Lili. I am six summers."

"And I am Saya Ani Anai," Saya finished. "I am the teacher. This is my school and this is our home."

The two little boys stared, overwhelmed.

"Won't you tell us your names?" Mara asked.

"Yes, tell us, tell us!" Lili said, clapping encouragement.

One of the boys took a deep breath. "I am Timma," he said. "I am five summers old, I think." He was the boy who had sliced open the purse. He had brown hair and dark skin. He was lean and looked very hungry, as if he had been giving most of the food he stole to the other boy.

"Welcome, Timma," Saya said.

"Yes, welcome!" Lili exclaimed. She grabbed him and hugged him tightly.

The students all turned to the other boy, but he was frozen. He looked up at Saya, on the verge of tears. He tugged on her robes until she leaned down to him. He cupped both hands around her ear and whispered.

"This is Beni," Saya said.

Another tug at her robes. More whispering.

"Beni is four summers old," Saya said.

"Welcome, Beni," they all said.

Lili tried to hug him too, but Beni shrieked and hid himself in Saya's robes again.

"You can be safe here," Saya told them. "There are no outsiders, no normals. This will be your home, where there will always be a roof to shelter under, and food to fill your bellies. A place for people like us to learn to be careful with our special gifts."

Saya went down to one knee. She put a hand on each of the boys' shoulders, looking them in the eyes. "Everyone here can bind the streams to render magick, just like you. The more you practice, the better you will become. But we must remain hidden. We must be invisible. You must never let anyone see you use your powers outside these walls. Not anyone. The normals would report you to the Priests. Do you understand?"

They both nodded.

Saya smiled. "You are both very lucky. It is a good thing that you are here with us now. It is never safe outside. Here you are always safe. Here you are home."

They nodded again.

Saya gave them a quick severe look. "There are words we all say every day. So that we remember." She turned to the other students. "Why do we hide who we are?"

"Because they hate us," all answered in unison.

"Who hunts us?" she asked.

"The Priests," they answered.

"What happens if we are seen?"

"We run."

"What happens if we are chased?"

"We hide."

"What happens if we are caught?"

"We burn."

They all bowed their heads for a silent moment, then were back to jeering and jesting with each other.

Adrani knelt down and gave both boys a strong hug. "Welcome. Today was your first day. Not so bad, was it?"

Timma and Beni both smiled. Everyone was clapping and laughing.

"Now, how about we have some supper?" Radir asked. "I don't know about the rest of you scoundrels, but I'm starving."

Lili hopped and clapped again.

Supper consisted of boiled greybeans, leek stew flavored with thyme, and a bit of the day's catch of fish, a cup of sweetmeal on the side.

And, of course, half her students were already out in the yard playing before Saya had even managed to wrangle a bowl for herself. She carried it out onto the porch and sat in the creaky chair. Qudra brought her sweet tea he had stolen from the markets that morning. It was warm, but then again everything was in Kasaban. She was so grateful she had no trouble enjoying it.

Lili and Aafi danced around the new boys, as the others ran and shrieked and giggled, playing chase-me around the trees and tossing clumps of dirt in each other's hair. And laughing. Endlessly laughing.

That was a gift worth more to Saya than gold.

Welcome Timma, she thought, her eyes glossing over. *Welcome Beni.*

She smiled. She had saved two more. Two more precious little ones who were now safe from burning.

There is always a chance tomorrow might be better. Sometimes tomorrow is today.

4

A Graveyard Of Joy

IT IS HARD TO LOVE something when it terrifies you.

Saya was terrified of Kasaban.

She was afraid of the place she was born.

Most days she was good at hiding it.

Today was not one of those days.

"Something troubles you," Terak said. The old Biss merchant tilted his head back and looked down his narrow nose at her. "Your smile is less."

"I have too many thoughts today," she said.

The room was so dark with all the windows shuttered that she half expected to see her thoughts dancing in the gloom. Twin candles were less than half of not enough to light even this small shop. But she was glad to be out of the light and the heat of the white sun, out of the choking dust, away from the eyes.

He glanced up at her, his hands holding a bottle and a dropper mere inches apart. "Something happens, yes?"

She shook her head, loosening the cords and lifting the flap on her coinpurse. "Not one thing. Many things. Worries. Where will the money come from? Our take at the pond was less than we needed. I have had to stretch. Tashim needs new boots. We need a new cup to replace the one Qudra broke, and Adrani needs pennysage for the pain. She celebrated her menarch this week."

"This is wonderful for her. Cause of celebrating."

"It is one more unexpected thing I do not have money for."

"Like this medicine I order for you?" He gestured to the corked golden-brown bottle he had tied an olive ribbon about with the name *chrisanthus oil* on it.

She nodded. "Like Aafi's medicine, yes."

"Is not cheap to import. Plague doctors of Malorin only makers."

"He cannot live without it," she said, the corners of her eyes drooping. "He will die."

"Is important. Why I cut you deal for this, yes." He smiled gap-toothed, his grey whiskers a sandpaper mask. He smoothed out a square of paper to wrap the bottle.

Saya felt her heart warm and her body swayed involuntarily, her eyes closing briefly. "Yes, and thank you so much. I know you did not have to."

He shrugged, his eyes returning to his work. "Your mother brought me much business. Always."

"My mother." She had intended to say more, but the words died on her tongue.

He kept smiling, but did not look up from his work. "She did not put heart on sleeve as you."

Saya smiled. She succeeded in holding back a tear. "That is my mother for you. People always used to ask me if she even knew how to laugh. They never believed me. But at home it was different. At home she laughed all the time. That was why I loved home so much. She could be who she really was there."

"Except one day," he said. "One day she cries. I remember this. Not long after she comes to buy pennysage first time for you."

"The day they took my brother."

He puffed his wrinkled lips out into a frown. "This I am sorry."

"It was my fault."

He paused what he was doing, let the paper uncurl, hands resting on the table, leaning against each other in resignation. "You must not think these thoughts."

"It is true."

"Fault, fault, what is this?" He raised his hands and danced them back and forth between them as if searching the air for the meaning. "Fault is always of many making. Never just one."

"I couldn't save him," she said, looking down and away, tucking her nose into her shoulder.

"The guilt of the one who lives."

"That was the first time my parents took me to the fires. My father made me watch them burn him."

His eyes sank and he frowned, but his hands went back to folding and rolling the old paper around the bottle, layer after layer, pulling it taught, smoothing out every lump. Saya was so glad for it. If her eyes did not have the purposeful motions of his hands to watch, they would have submerged into an ocean of tears not even the desert could dry away.

"I loved my father. I don't blame him. He was so angry. He was in pain."

"He should not have taken you to see that."

She reached out a hand, elbow straight, like a child. "Same day next month?"

He nodded, sad smile, close-lipped. He reached out and placed the wrapped bottle in her hand. It crinkled against her palm. "Take good care," he said.

"I will."

"Next time bring one of the little ones with you," he suggested. "Your mind is better when they are near."

"I will," she promised, though already she rued having to tell the other ten small students that they had to stay home while another had a chance to roam. She stuffed the bottle safely into her shoulder bag, pressing it into the center of the rolled-up scarf Khersas had given her.

When she opened the door, darkness vanished. She walked into a wall of white. The light splashed over her, like a wash of flame across her face, a savage rushing current, scraping her skin. She nearly drowned in the heat. Within seconds she felt a sheen of sweat everywhere at once. Thankfully, there was a humble breeze, the air licking at her skin, peeling her sweat away and leaving a tiny fraction of cool in its place. Before she made it halfway down the street her mouth was dry.

She spent as little time as she could in the markets lining the street. None of them could put anything out unless a thick canvas canopy was stretched across their tables of goods. Much of the fruits were weathered, and some inedible, but Xarla always saved one good calpas fruit in the back for her.

The stoneware cup was even more expensive than she thought, prices higher from all the demand caused by the fresh batch of Ministry acolytes rotating into Kasaban to continue their crusade and spread their poison religion to every inch of the basin.

From Madinas to Nabena, from the dune seas of Rhodas to the gates of Naphesus, once they had it all they would finally make the push into Holy Sephalon, where the eldest gods dwelled, the place their prophecies said they must control before they could usher in the days of light that accompanied the return of their Lord of Truth.

Saya had heard the stories. Refugees from Madinas spoke of massacres. Mercenaries from Rhodas claimed that entire neighborhoods were razed to the ground to punish a single offense. Those strong enough to survive the trek from Besembria told tales of how the Priests had left a hellscape of lawless anguish in their wake.

Yet their appetite remained unfulfilled.

Whispers in the markets and in line at the poorchanger often said that for the Priests of the Ministry to legitimize their empire, they first needed to conquer the ancient lands of the oldest gods. The needed to conquer Holy Sephalon, sacred to their undying master. If they did so, the whole world would tremble before them.

And they could not begin the sacred war for Holy Sephalon they craved without first subjugating Kasaban.

Saya had seen companies of soldiers march through on their way to the fighting, and seen many wounded return. She had witnessed conscriptions of her own people into the holy armies, dragged off to unseen wars in distant lands, never to be seen again. She had lived through enough reprisals to learn the futility of rebellion.

She turned at the sandstone bakery and threaded a narrow alley where the walls were covered with the chalk outlines of the shrines to the old gods, the ones whose statues had been destroyed, declared illegal to pray to. The faithful came here now, to worship outlines in the shape of their gods in this narrow space.

The Priests could not comprehend any importance in two dimensions, so what they took away in three dimensions, the people recreated in two, putting them in a place no Priest would ever deign to walk. They hid their faith in plain sight. In pictures. In love.

Saya's heart leapt with the pure strength it took to keep loving when everything around you told you it could not be so. In this one alley, among the gods whose names she didn't even know, she felt safe, she felt free, she felt alive. For one brief moment she knew peace. Where she had nowhere to go, no one to be. And she could dance and skip and close her eyes without fear.

This narrow rotten alley was freedom.

When she came out the other side she felt renewed, refreshed. She had what she needed and then some. She was ready to be what her students needed, something more than just a person, a teacher.

She stopped by the Moneychanger's compound. She waited patiently in the line for the poor, the one that led to a single small table where a man in a chair would convert coins and currencies and denominations. He was flanked by two men with heavy truncheons. They seemed bored. No one would ever touch the poorchanger. Everyone of low standing in Kasaban needed this line to be here. The one who thieved or raised their hand in anger to the poorchanger man would be the one torn apart by the angry mob this line would become.

Never raise your hand to the poorchanger man, her father always used to say. It was the beginning of a rhyme, but he never told her the rest of it.

The large bodyguard who minded the iron gate of the walled patio leading deep into the Moneychanger compound was another story. He kept glancing suspiciously at her, at all of them, as if at any moment they intended to rush the gate and rob the place. The amount of money within the vault was more than enough that someone might be tempted to chance being torn limb from limb by the mob.

Saya just rolled her eyes at him.

By the time she reached the head of the line she had been standing in the sun for so long she was swimming in sweat. Her sleeve was dappled wet where she had blotted away beads of it rolling down her brow.

She changed out the silvers Beni and Timma had thieved, receiving the equal value in full coppers. Half the vendors in the poormarkets she visited would not even accept payment in silvers. It made her nervous even to hold so much money in public, like a sign floating above her, following her everywhere, telling everyone how much money she had to steal. Even though it was near the same amount of money, she felt safer carrying copper.

She finished her shopping in the poormarkets by early afternoon, well ahead of schedule, winding her way through the tables and carts on the edge of the city, a place where she could look up and see Kasaban's namesake, the high mountain of Sora Kasab, rising alone from the flat desert floor. She bought more fishing line, and new soles to sew into Tashim's boots, blackroot for Noqer to chew on, and a tiny tray of peppermint candies for everyone to share.

She danced her way out into the Old King's Square, still well kept from the days of ancient Adumbar, the *empire without limit*, a place where people gathered in the shade of orange trees to talk and share news while standing upon green grass, serenaded by the sweet sibilance of rushing irrigation channels. They were each but eight inches wide, yet they were the largest running rivers Saya had ever seen.

If she closed her eyes she could even pretend it was not surrounded by guards with long, sharp spears and knives, ready to take a hand if any of the poorest of Kasaban tried to steal some of its water. She had been standing beneath a fat orange at the end of a branch for more than three breaths already, which was itself enough to earn sidelong glances from more than one of the ivory-robed sentinels.

If she had not had her own orange tree within the red brick walls of her home, she might have been tempted to try her luck with snatching one of these.

She paused there, taking breath after breath, feeling the sunshine and watching the children play. *Oh, how good it would feel to watch my children play out here one day.* Safe. Carefree.

She watched a small boy share his licorice rope with a little girl through a quilt of the branches of three different trees. Two older boys battled each other with sticks, while two even younger girls played chase-me around them, diving under their swings.

She saw a girl perhaps only a few years younger than her whispering to a boy and turning crimson-faced before leaning in for an awkward and delicate kiss when no one was looking.

One boy, with a scar above his lip, bare but for a linen vest as skinny as he was, snuck up behind two of his friends and mashed one half of a cream pastry in one's face. He sprinted away so fast, Saya barely saw him hide behind a stone bench to watch them.

The pastry-faced boy furiously wiped cream out of his eyes, and slapped the other, assuming him to be the prankster. The other shoved him back, and before she could blink they were slapping each other silly. The guilty boy laughed all the while.

Saya could not help but chuckle. It felt so good. Laughter was so hard sometimes in Kasaban, at least away from home. But she so easily saw the face of Qudra on the prankster, and Aafi and Sotta slapping each other. The two sword fighters were Raba and Faloush. Tana and Lili chased each other all about. Tashim shared his candy with Serine. Adrani traded tongue with Radir.

A warm breeze suddenly buffeted her, and just like that, the faces were gone, changed back into the strangers they belonged to. Saya was alone again. The square was an alien world once more.

This place is not my home. It will never be my home. I should know better than to daydream.

The ground she stood upon was not that far from the place where they took her brother, ripping him right out of her arms. Only three streets over was the small house with the large front window she had grown up in, the window through which they had spotted her father's afterglow on the night he drank too much bitterwine and brandy and forgot to be careful. The belltower she could see rising above the two-story roofs sat across from the library where her mother had hidden her in a cabinet when they kicked down the door and took her away.

This city wasn't home. This place was the graveyard of her joy.

It was time to go back to her true home, the hidden, fortified compound she had dedicated so much of her life and strength into building for her students.

She had lost someone on the streets, so she made a place that was apart from the streets. She had lost someone through a pane of glass, betrayed by a window, so she made a place that had no windows. She had lost someone through a door, so she built a place with no doors. That was her school. It was more than just a place. It was her. The manifestation of her compulsive need to protect at all costs.

Though it was small, it was hers, her toil, her time, her sweat, her work...and her responsibility to protect. No matter what she had to do. No matter how low she had to scrape.

What she could not do with physical strength she would see done with her mind. What she could not do with force, she would make so with her preparation and foresight. What hope she could not create with her weak magick, she would purchase with her body.

I am coming, she promised her home.

She breezed past the trees and coasted through the people, ready at last to return home.

But something wasn't quite right. She felt a prickling on her neck, the same sensation as the day Khersas never came home.

She slowed, eyes leaping about frantically, searching for the source of the sensation. What was it? What was she feeling? She could not explain it to herself. She only knew something was wrong.

The people around her kept walking, kept talking, kept laughing or arguing. Children cried out in delight and babies squealed in the distance. Birdsong. The hammers of smiths hard at work. Her ears heard only the normal, the expected.

Her eyes captured only bobbing heads and drifting robes crisscrossing the square.

It was all so ordinary that her eyes lost focus, the moving people fading into the background. Once movement became her background, the motionless leapt to her attention.

Her eyes settled on the only thing that was not moving—a man in a tattered brown coat, goggles strapped to his head by leather bands, lenses like foggy glass. He did not move, or make a sound, his teeth bared as if his mouth was unsure if it was chewing or screaming. He stared at her as though she was the only person in the world.

Her body turned to ice, her sweat disappeared, leaving her dry and cold.

He just stared. As if he was waiting for her to do something.

Glassdog.

She never dreamed they would be as terrifying to look at as this man was. They were madmen, it was said, driven insane by the constant hazy world permeated by magick their augmented eyes saw day and night. The goggles were ranum crystal lenses, same as the ones in the Jecker monocles the Glasseyes used to hunt.

They were not rational investigators like the Glasseyes. They did not plan, or evaluate evidence. They were bloodhounds, their sole purpose to spot any hint of residual afterglow in the air, or on clothes, or hands, or doorknobs. They were only there to see. And when they saw what they were looking for, they would cry out for the Priests to come.

Saya's heart thudded back to life. She could almost feel the relief oozing through her blood. She remembered she had not used any magick in more than a day. She would be clean. Pure. Normal. He could stare at her for hours, from inches away and he would never see the stain of afterglow anywhere near her.

Knowing what he was calmed her. The knowing alone banished much of the fear. But then the implications began to mount. They must have been having trouble finding more magi to burn. Why else would they bring in such special weapons? And expensive. She had heard each of the polished lenses might as well have been made of diamonds.

They must be desperate to find more of us. That meant those like Saya who yet lived were getting better at hiding themselves. *When we are all gone, when we are all turned to flame, will they keep burning people? Will they take normals off the street and pretend they are like me just so they can keep the fires going?*

She did not doubt it.

The Glassdog kept staring.

She now needed to return home faster than ever. To warn Adrani and Radir before they went out as thieves for their evening pocket-runs. To warn the children that the Glassdogs were here, and would always be watching.

She wondered if before long it would not be safe for any of the children to leave the safe walls of home at all.

She turned away, taking the first of many steps down the dusty white streets of Kasaban. But before her foot could even fall her eyes swept over a gilded mask.

A Priest towered over her, face hidden behind a mask of burnished gold. The lidless black eyeholes gazed at her and all through her, staring beyond space and time, seeing her whole life, seeing her future all in one horrifying glance. The mouth hole, a perfect circle, screamed through history, making her most distant ancestors shiver.

Horror squirmed through her. The pure white robes, as white as the powder dust of the desert, were like a wall before her, the hooded head a boulder, ready to fall from above and crush the existence out of her.

She did not scream. She wanted to. But blessedly her mouth failed. Her breath gusted out of her lungs like the kick of a mule. Every muscle of her face felt pinched and twisted, held taut by fishhooks.

"I know your face," the gold mask said. The voice was muted within the mask, but fierce and cruel and with such presence that it was as if her ear was inside his mouth whenever he spoke.

Saya's skin melted and froze and melted again in the horror of that statement. *I know.* Being known by them was doom.

"Do you not speak the true tongue?" he asked. But with them even a question was a threat.

"I do speak it," Saya said.

The golden mask never changed, frozen in scream. There was no way to judge his expression, no way to tell how much danger she was in. His mouth moved behind it, his eyes scanned from across the unfathomable gulf of the eyeholes.

"That is good. We will not be forced to submit you for pacification in Madinas."

Madinas. One city closer to their empire. The last one they laid claim to before coming to Kasaban—crushing rebellions, purging magi, and colonizing it with peoples from all over the Corien Empire. The place where Khersas had been born.

"Do you know who I am?" the Priest asked.

She shook her head.

"The name given to me is Sevastin Karda. The honored title bestowed upon me is Most Holy Guardian General of the Sacred Light. I am the guiding force of this crusade. I am the reason for everything that happens here."

"I have done nothing."

"The people here know me by a different name," he said. "Perhaps you have heard it. The White Death of Kasaban."

Saya noticed a tiny mark beside one eyehole, an engraving, the shape of a tear.

Burner of children.

Saya felt her body dissolve. Her skin became a shell, her bones and organs liquified by fear. She was surprised her tongue obeyed when she spoke. "I just want to go on my way."

"Would you like to know why I know your face?" His voice was soft and smooth and glazed sweet, but there was such weight behind it, a depth such that she feared to hear words spoken in his lowest tones.

She blinked. She could not keep her teeth from gnawing the insides of her lips. She dared not turn her back on him. Not even to run away. "Why?"

"Because you were seen in the crowd of holy witnesses to the beautiful cleansing flames of the Lord of Truth. You watched us bring purity to this place, to root out the darkness."

Her eyes burned, trying to close. "I like knowing I live in a place that is clean."

"And where is it that you live?"

"I do not wish to bother you," she said. "I will be on my way."

"To where?"

She choked on her tongue.

Sevastin Karda leaned forward, looming above her like a raincloud. "I like to walk these streets myself. I like to see with my own eyes the tireless work of my brothers, and the fruits of their labor." He paused. "And I like to look at the ordinary people. Like you. The ones who interest me the most are the ones who stare. And during the last excruciation ceremony I watched you stare until the last one crisped."

"I watch. You want us to watch, don't you? Isn't that why you show us?"

"We want you to *know*. Knowledge is the path to truth. And we worship the Lord of Truth who is the Lord of Light which is the place where all magick comes from."

"I know who you worship. It is all that remains to worship here." She could feel the little tickle in her mind that meant he was touching the source of magick. He had not plunged into the Slipstream yet, not even begun to reach for whichever streams would answer to him, not even used his pattern to open the door to that infinite white light of possibility, but even the mere act of leaning against it, pressing on the boundary with his mind was enough that, standing so close to him, she could sense it.

He is ready. He expects me to be a threat. If I reach for any of my magick, he will kill me with his own before I even finish binding streams.

Sevastin Karda stared at her through the empty eyeholes of the golden mask. "Lies are born of secrets. Secrets live in darkness. Darkness masks knowledge, and hides truth. In the light, truth is shown to us. Only by doing away with the darkness of secrets shall we find the light of truth. Once all the secrets of this world have been obliterated, the Lord of Truth will return. They say no one knows what the Days of Light are. But we do. We have always known. It means it is the time of his return, when he brings our world and the world of light together as one. Righteous and whole. Lies grow like weeds in our midst. Even the smallest lie is a sin. Even the tiniest of secrets threatens your soul. Tell me your secrets."

"I have none. I am just a poor woman living in Kasaban, trying to make my way. That is all. I swear it."

"Everyone in Kasaban has secrets. I will have yours."

"I mean no trouble," she said. "Please."

He did not move from her path.

"My errands..." she started to say.

"Yes. What have you there?"

She leaned away from him, both hands holding the flap of her bag closed.

But then another man appeared behind her. He wore the same white robes, but sheltered beneath no hood, and hid behind no mask. An acolyte of the Ministry, the lowest tier of their accepted. That meant he had magick as well, just like this Priest.

His face was young, features sharp, skin as pale as snow, hair a red sandstorm crowning his head. His eyes were ice blue. He was beautiful, the kind of young man women would melee for, that artists would scramble to immortalize in paint and marble.

The acolyte tore the bag off her shoulder, and he and the Priest plunged hands carelessly into it.

Her eyes bulged. "No, please. There is nothing in there. Nothing of value. Please." She reached out a hand to stop him.

"You do not touch me," the beautiful young acolyte said, slapping her hand aside and carrying on.

She pulled her hand back, and her stomach settled into empty fright. "Just some things for my household. Food, medicine."

They ignored her. Sevastin tossed the loaf of bread aside, while the acolyte tumbled the calpas fruits into the dust. They poured out Noqer's blackroot into the dirt, caking each piece white.

"Please stop," she said. *Please don't ruin the only little joys my children will know in this place. Please.* She tried to will them to stop, to grow bored, to move on, to leave her alone.

Her will was not strong enough.

"Are you feeling angry?" Sevastin asked.

Saya gritted her teeth. "Please stop."

The faceless Priest nodded to the acolyte. "Continue."

He dropped the other supplies out, reveling in the pain twisting across her face.

"Why?" she asked. "I haven't done anything. I swear by Holy Juna. I take my knees for you. Please."

"Fall to your knees then," Sevastin agreed.

Saya dropped to her knees so hard that pain streaked down her legs. "I am nothing. Not worth your time please." *Please don't find the medicine.*

He dropped the new cup. It shattered on the stone street.

Saya began to cry. It was such a little thing. Nothing to them. Why did they need to take her things? Why did they need to ruin what little there was for her to have?

"Are you angry yet?" Sevastin asked. "Show me how angry you are."

What does he want? Is he testing me? Why? Then she glanced across the square and saw that the Glassdog was still there, watching her.

They are trying to make me use magick. They are trying to make me slip.

Sevastin took out a handful of her coins and hurled them to the ground. They scattered in all directions, bouncing and rolling among the feet of the people in the street. The people reached down and chased them with glee, snatching up one or two, scooping them up and pocketing them and running off.

"Please," she begged, her knees grinding on stone. "Please. It is all I have. We will starve."

"Who is *we?*" Sevastin asked.

No. I should not have said anything. I should not have opened my mouth.

At last he reached in and plucked out the bottle wrapped in paper. He held it up between thumb and forefinger, the mask never turning away from her face.

He let it go.

Saya lunged forward. Her elbows cracked on the street, tearing her skin. Her fingers outstretched just barely made it far enough to cushion the bottle of chrisanthus oil, saving it from shattering within its paper wrapping.

"Please let me go," she begged from the ground, her body stretched across hot stone. "Please."

Please, Holy Juna, shine your light for me.

Another Priest suddenly arrived. He whispered in Sevastin's ear. Without a word, he motioned to the acolyte. Her bag was dropped. Their feet moved on past her, grinding sand into the ground on either side of her face.

They left like a breath of summer heat.

She sat up, and tucked the bottle back into the bag. She scooped up what little coin had not been stolen. The bread was still there. All but one of the calpas fruit had split open. The blackroot was salvageable with a little water and patience. She could not save the cup. And the money that was now gone was irreplaceable.

Once everything was in her bag she rose to her feet.

She stood there, shuddering, chest heaving, heart bursting, gasping for the smallest sip of air. Their absence did nothing to limit the fear they engendered in her. She felt frozen, blood full of ice. The heat hammered her skin but she could not sweat.

She felt a dull thump against her sandals. She looked down.

Two of the dunemakers had buried her feet up the ankles in white sand and dust, and now thumped her feet with their heavy push brooms, hitting her again and again until she staggered back into the wall, feet vanishing into a mountain range of white powder, clearing the clean street center for the people who deserved it, the people of wealth and means.

With what coins she had managed to scrape off the street she returned to the poormarkets to replace the pennysage they had stolen and the cup they had broken.

Her face was swollen with tears and terror. They had taken so much. She had lost half the coin to the crowd, and still more to re-purchase the lost items. She did not know how they would ever make up the difference. Even if the take from the pond and the fresh coin from the nightly pocket-runs set records each and every day until the end of the month, she still did not think she would have enough to pay Jacobas his fee.

She bit her lip until it bled. Her mind raced to think of a way to duplicate the lost income. *If I make my own runs. If I let*

Mara and Tashim go out on runs of their own even though they are so young. If I can trust Noqer not to let his anger get the better of him, he can go out, too. But with the Glassdogs on the streets, the risk was so much higher than it had ever been.

She stumbled back home in a daze. She slid through the windows and doors like melting butter, flowing down the secret winding ways she always used to throw off pursuit. She dripped down the ladders, oozed along the sewer tunnel, and trickled up the rope ladder, bubbling out of the storm grate.

Before she could even catch her breath, the children were already running up to her, cheering and clapping. They were so happy. They were so free. They did not have to know what was happening outside these walls.

Saya tried to suck all the tears back up into her eyes, pretending to have a mote of dust in her eyelid to buy the time to wipe them dry.

I will not let them know. They deserve so much love and happiness. They must never see it. They must not see what I have seen.

They wanted to dance. They wanted to sing. They wanted her smile.

She felt like her mind was dissolving. *I can't do this. I can't be here. I can't.*

She forced a smile well enough to fool them all, and excused herself upstairs to her bedroom, letting them all gather to eat supper. Radir and Adrani and Mara took charge and soon everyone had a bowl and a spoon and plenty to fill their bellies.

Saya listened to them from her room upstairs, hiding in her blankets, looking out the window onto the little yard below, with its little orange tree and its cedars, and its lone willow, and the poplar around the side, and the little shed Radir had claimed as his room, all surrounded by four safe walls of pretty red bricks.

She heard echoes of the children joking and rambling and careening from one conversation to the next as they ate. It came to her in chirps under her closed door, and in echoes from out in the yard. She did not need to understand their noisy chatter though, only to know it was there, to experience the awareness of their presence. That was enough.

She was overjoyed. She was terrified. She was full of love. She was empty and alone. The stars came out as the sun set. Saya buried her face in her pillow, hiding from them so that they would not see her tears.

On days like this she missed Khersas more than any other. She felt pulled in so many directions at once that she thought her body was splitting into a thousand pieces. He had always known how to keep the pieces of her together until she could be herself again. She needed him and she would never see him again. He was not here to be a blanket for her heart the way these blankets were for her body. He could not be that for her ever again...ever since the day they had taken him away.

She missed him. She missed him desperately. She needed his strength, his warmth, his wisdom. She thought about him every day, though she tried not to. If her mind lingered a little too long on the thought of him, she would burst into tears. She could not allow her students to see that. She had to be strong for the children. She was their best hope. She was their only hope.

She locked her door, pulled the blankets over her head, and lay in the dark alone.

5

Teacher

"WHY DO WE STEAL?" Tana asked, and Saya was not sure she knew the answer. There were so many reasons. How to choose one? She had been taught to hide and steal when she was not much older than Tana was now.

"We steal because we must," Saya said.

"But why must we?" Tana pressed. She sat cross-legged in the shade provided by the cedar tree, her little ivory robe dirty from playing in the yard the day before.

"We must eat," Saya answered.

"But Noqer and Aafi bring us fish from the pond," Tana argued. "And we get oranges from the orange tree."

"Yes," Saya agreed. "But Noqer and Aafi cannot catch grain and rice and oil and bread and squash and calpas fruit at the pond, and we cannot grow any here." She thumped the dirt with her fist and looked up at the four red brick walls surrounding them.

Here Saya was safe, with no door or window to the outside world, save for the drain, and even that was covered with canvas and leaves. The high brick walls provided protection from passing eyes and the merciless driving desert winds. The yard smelled of orange blossoms and cedar sap. Her mother's and father's favorites respectively. She thought of that every time one of her students brought her to frustration.

"Does Noqer steal the fish from the pond?" Lili asked, plopping herself down beside Tana. "Will the pond be mad at him?"

"No," Saya smiled. "The pond gives us its bounty for free, but the normals who grow the grain and vegetables are not as charitable as the pond. They expect to be given something in exchange."

"Coins," Lili said.

"And we must pay Jacobas his fee, so he will keep our home a secret from the other warren-bosses and the Priests."

"But isn't it wrong to steal?" Tana asked. "We are not supposed to take each other's things without asking."

"Yes," Lili agreed. "It makes you mad."

Saya yawned. "It is okay to steal from normals. They would take what is ours and burn us if they had the chance. It is their own fault. In the world that they have made for us, we have no choice. You do not need to feel sorry for them."

"Is it okay to kill someone?" Raba asked, coming to join them. "Noqer says we should be allowed to kill normals, too."

"Noqer needs to be more careful about the things he says. We do not want to kill anyone."

"But what if it is to protect us?" Raba asked. "Is it okay then? Noqer says it is all right to kill someone like Jacobas."

"Noqer!" Saya called out, terse, angry. *He should not be filling their heads with such thoughts. He should not be having such thoughts himself.*

Several moments passed and Noqer had not appeared.

"He is in his room, I think," Raba said. "Practicing."

Saya released a long sigh. "We never want to harm anyone. We must always plan in such a way that we are never faced with that choice."

"Not even Jacobas?" Tana asked.

Saya nodded. "Especially not Jacobas."

"But you hate him," Lili said. "He is ugly and disgusting."

"Sometimes we must put up with things we do not like to save ourselves from things we like even less."

"Like the Priests?" Tana asked.

"Yes, like the Priests."

Saya banished Raba to practice by the orange tree, and she sent Lili inside to pour herself some water. The poor girl could not remember to keep herself hydrated even a little.

Once she and Tana were alone again, she appealed to the child to focus. "Close your eyes, Tana. Try again. Concentrate."

Saya wiped beads of sweat from her brow with one ivory cuff. She closed her eyes and exhaled. She repeated this three times, gazing up at the row of towering cedars spearing the sky, vaulting like cathedrals, shading the citrus trees for the hottest half of the day.

Her back had been stiff for hours, her legs sore from sitting cross-legged in the dirt, an itch terrorizing her right buttock such that no matter how she tried to scratch it, her robes clung too tight to her skin to alleviate it. Standing up to resettle her robes would have been to admit defeat. So here she was.

She made a tight frown and shook her head at Tana. The girl had very nearly pulled the proper streams together to render a two-dimensional shape for the first time. For as long as she had lived here and longer still, she had only been able to bind together the most basic streams, the kind most other students mastered when they were still toddling about.

And now *finally* Tana had almost brought two lines together into a plane, would have, if not for her interminable distractedness. Saya blessed the stars that she could keep the girl's focus for five minutes.

"Tana," Saya whispered.

The girl's eyes snapped back to Saya, wide and full of fear.

"Stop trying to see if Qudra is noticing you," Saya said. "You must learn to do this. Timma has *already* learned this." Saya had paired Timma with Tana, as they both were able to render slice-lines that had enough strength to at least cut fabric.

Tana looked at her feet, bare on the cobbles of the courtyard, her shame palpable. She sniffled, wiping snot from her nose with one little fist.

"Aya Jaytat," Saya said, exasperated. She looked across the yard at the awning shading the porch. She closed her eyes again. Another breath. She listened to the drips of condensation from her glass of water as they plopped onto the stones beneath the wicker table. She licked her lips involuntarily. *I should have brought the water over here. Why did I leave it? Fool.*

"I can't do it," Tana protested.

Saya held up one finger. "You can't do it *yet.*"

"I'll never do it. Everyone else gets better but never me."

Saya scrunched her cheek and raised her eyebrows. "Both of those things are untrue. You *will* get better if you try. And you are not the only one who struggles."

Tana waved her hand all around, gesturing at the other students dispersed about the yard, clustered about the other cedars, beneath the orange tree, and against the eaves of Radir's shed. "They are all better."

"Many are older than you. You will see how great a difference a few years makes."

"Serine and Lili are younger than me. And now Beni and Timma."

Saya folded her arms. "Is that what this is about? The little new boys?"

Tana folded her arms now, too, still crying. "It was bad enough when it was two, now there are four little babies who are all better than me."

Saya looked over her shoulder and wagged her finger in a circle, mimicking Tana's disgruntled outburst. "Look around at them. All of them. All of them struggle, all of them wish they were better, no matter their age."

Tashim and Serine practiced making shapes in the air—spheres and circles respectively. "See how Serine strives to be as good as Tashim?"

Faloush demonstrated the crafting of two-dimensional walls, and Raba showed off how he created invisible cubes. "Watch how Faloush looks at Raba with such admiration."

She pointed to Aafi, the little frictioneer, and Qudra working with stress and tension renders beneath the orange tree. Adrani struggled with streams of buoyancy trying to keep a toy boat afloat, while Sotta buffeted it with renders of wave upon wave of surging air pressure. Mara ran through her drills of rendering changes in light and darkness, waiting for Saya to finish with Tana to guide her. Beni was supposed to be with Noqer behind the old shed, playing his intriguing gravitational talent against Noqer's skill with mass and density, but, of course, Noqer was late coming down from his room again.

Lili tried cheerfully to demonstrate her skill of altering the porousness of surfaces but was too excited to concentrate, failing to render anything at all.

Tana is not the only one with concentration issues.

Saya smiled. "There is only one thing you can know for sure is true about anyone who is really good at something."

"What?"

"They used to be terrible at it."

Tana smiled. "Not really though."

"Really though. Everything. Everyone. Even me. None of us begins knowing what we are doing. We only get there because we practice. We get there because we try."

"I am afraid I will fail." Tana's shoulders sagged.

Saya lowered her face, and turned her eyes up until they looked through hers. "The only way to fail is not to try."

"It just seems like forever to get there," Tana complained. "It would take a million years for me to be as good as Raba, or as good as you."

"The streams will come to you when you are ready. The more you practice the better your concentration will be. The better your concentration the stronger you will become. The stronger you become, the more and mightier streams will reveal themselves to you whenever you touch the source. The more streams you can bind together, the more you will need to practice to keep your concentration always improving to manage them all. It is a cycle. It never ends. You or I will never reach a point where we stop getting better. Unless we stop trying. Do you understand?"

Tana nodded.

"You are at the very beginning of what you will be able to do, Tana. But that is where we all started. None of us were born as masters. None of us are masters now. We are all students. Even me. The teacher is a student. It is always this way. Great things come from small beginnings."

That was how it had been for Saya. Equal measures of exhilaration and fear the first time she touched the Slipstream, dipped inside, called for streams and those streams actually answered.

Binding them into a render had been so easy, like taking a step, like those first weak streams *wanted* to come to her. And every time she grew stronger, her renders locked more fully in reality. Different shapes, different sizes, rendering further and further away from her body with confidence.

Saya felt like she was watching herself as a child when she looked at Tana.

The most simple tangible thing to exist required at least a position in space, a shape, and a duration. Those were the first streams that would come to any user of magick when they wandered into the source for the first time. The streams would be weak—lasting a little more than a second, the shape of a single point, a position within arm's reach because anything further away than that and they might pass out from the exertion.

If they could make each of those three streams come together at once, and focus long enough to bind them together, they would have a render. Even when they could, their strength and concentration would barely hold. The magnitude of the render in reality would be a hairsbreadth away from winking out of existence.

Most magi would then find the streams of mass available to them, and once they learned to bind them with the others, they could make their shapes have weight, and become tactile. Then they could add direction and motion. Tana was not there yet, but she was close.

"I want to do better, Sayani. I want to make you proud of me. I just feel like I will never be good."

Saya hid her tears. She wanted to lock her in a relentless embrace, but she held back. *I must be her teacher first.* "You say you want to be as good as me. I am a lightbender. Do you know what that means?"

Tana shook her head.

"It means I can render shapes, many shapes, all different sizes and angles and dimensions, but they will only affect the travel of light—through reflection, refraction, or diffusion. None of them will ever have any mass. None will ever be physically tangible. I can never strike a blow against someone with one of my renders, nor can I shield someone from an attack. That is something you will always be able to do, that I can never do. Streams of mass and strength will come to you as you grow, Tana, but they will never come to me. I can make shapes like Tashim or Raba, but anyone could walk right through mine, hear sounds passing unchallenged through them."

"There is truly something I can do that you cannot?" Tana was amazed.

Saya nodded. "Each of us has something that makes us special. It is up to us to find out what that is, and how to nurture it. Look at the others. Stop trying to be them. You can never be them, and they can never be you, no matter how hard they try."

"Yes, Sayani."

"I want you to keep trying, Tana, because I want to see the smile on your face when your streams start to show themselves. I want to share your joy when they come to answer your call."

"You make them sound like they are alive," Tana said.

Saya smiled. "I like to think of the streams of magick that way. It makes it easier for me to focus on finding them when my mind dips into the Slipstream. Binding them together to render into reality is easier for me when I think of them as members of a little family, coming back together after a long time apart. Or you can think of it the way Raba does, that they are just pieces of possibility that we can use to alter reality. Just numbers in mathematical equations that we can change to suit our needs."

A new kind of smile premiered on Tana's face. "I like it the way you do it. Where they are all friends, living in the Slipstream, waiting for me to visit."

"If doing so clears your mind and focuses your attention, then that is how we will always look at it. Right now, you are afraid to try, because you are afraid you won't get any better. If you don't try you don't have to face it. Am I right?"

Tana looked up at her, as if *known* at last for the first time. "How did you know?"

"Because that is the same thing that I did when I was little. I told myself I would never get any better and so I never tried. But trying is the only way we ever can get any better. Once I realized this, I stopped being that scared little girl. Now I am your teacher. Someday you will be someone's teacher, too."

Tana smiled wide, her eyes looking up at the pure blue sky, tracing newly realized scenes from her future into its vastness.

She reached out and lifted Tana's chin up by her thumb and forefinger, staring hard into her eyes, pale blue like an afternoon sky. "Do you want to improve?"

Tana nodded vigorously, her red hair dancing and sparkling in the sun like tongues of flame "Yes. I want to so badly."

"You will. Don't be afraid. You will be the best of us someday. But only if you do the work. You have to want it. You have to try."

"I will. I promise."

Saya rose to her feet, brushing dirt off her robes. "Now we break for water." She started toward the porch and its promised cup.

Tana kept silent. She glanced down nervously.

Saya watched her for a moment, then said, "You forgot to bring your water, didn't you?"

Tana might as well have been a solid block from the ice den for all she moved.

"Well, go and get it," Saya said, dismissing her with a wave of her hand.

Tana ran across the yard and threw the door open, her feet plodding down the hall, past the shoe wall and fishing rods, up the stairs to the room she shared with Serine and Lili.

Saya rolled her eyes. *If that girl tried half as hard at her training as she did pretending to be a princess in some imaginary kingdom, she would best all of us.*

Saya floated to the wooden bench, thirst making the ground feel like air beneath her feet, her mind only aware of that cup of cool water. Her eyes would have licked the condensation off the outside of it if they could. The way the desert stole the moisture from her, a cup like this was better than any candy sweets.

Her fingers took to the cup like a vice even before she sat down, the rim already at her lips before the backs of her knees raked the edge of the bench, wood smoothed from decades of use. Her lips parted for sweet water before her hips met wood. The seat of the bench creaked, as delicious liquid spilled into her mouth, flashing across her teeth, sliding around her cheeks, and running down her throat. Always a sip at first, just for a moment, just to savor, before the thirst turned her ravenous, gulping and swallowing down the entire cup in a desperate frenzy.

When it was empty, she set the cup down, embarrassed. But she felt sated, and it settled her empty belly. She had been skipping the midday meal to spare every bit she could to scrape together enough for another month, and another fee for Jacobas.

She gazed over at one of the cedars, where Tashim and Serine were practicing spheres and circles. Tashim seemed even more patient than Saya herself sometimes, at least when it came to little Serine, calmly critiquing her attempts.

She had nearly managed to render a complete sphere three times under his tutelage, though she had not been able to hold her concentration long enough to complete them, or place any mass within them. Serine swore to Tashim that she would make him proud with a complete sphere before the summer was over.

Noqer at last sauntered by now that an opportunity to be a mischief emerged. He waved his hand right through the failed ones and laughed. Serine scowled and burned holes with her gaze through the back of his tattered orange coat, her hands on her hips like a grumpy grandmother.

Tana still had not returned, and Saya began to tap her bare foot impatiently. The girl had most certainly run into Faloush and Raba and become distracted all over again.

Aya Jaytat.

A flash of motion whipped past her.

"Give it back!" Mara cried, flying across the porch after Raba. The gust of air in their wake was a lonely welcome breeze.

"No!" Raba chortled over his shoulder, his red vest trailing after him like flapping wings. "You said if I could guess where the last apple was then I could have the stone flute for today."

"You cheated!" Mara accused, tripping over her own robes and stumbling, nearly falling, spinning to keep herself upright, soaring across the yard after him.

Raba ducked under branches, weaved around cedars, and leapt over roots, using all the reckless speed his eight-year-old legs could churn out. Each time he passed another hurdle, he looked over his shoulder.

But Mara was always right there with him. She was clumsy and awkward and her robes inhibited her, but she had seen twelve summers, and her legs were more than long enough to make up for it.

Raba laughed over his shoulder at her, but when he turned his eyes ahead, his face collided with a plump orange. His head snapped back, arms flailing, his legs running out from under him. He flopped like a sack on the grass, the stone flute bouncing out of his hand. Mara snatched it up, giggling.

Saya heard a devious snicker. She glanced to her left and saw Noqer leaning up against the wall beside her bench, elbow resting in one hand, his other fingers pretending to stroke his nonexistent whiskers and smiling like a clever little villain.

He could easily have bound streams to decrease the mass of the orange at this distance. But he didn't. Poor Raba. Saya chuckled a bit to herself.

Mara reached for the flute, but Tashim suddenly rendered a sphere in the air before his hand. It was invisible but Saya heard Lili shriek from within the house and come barreling down the stairs.

Lili could always feel the ripples of stream-binding in the Slipstream faster than anyone she had ever known. It was as if she felt the ripples before they actually happened. Even Saya, sitting directly beside Tashim, did not feel the subtle tingling in her nerves until half a second later.

Tashim bound streams into his sphere—size of a marble, shape of a sphere, mass equal to a palmstone, and velocity of a diving jaybird. He set it in motion by flicking one of his fingers.

Tashim was nothing if not precise in every way. And binding streams was no different. When he wanted a sphere to fly in a certain direction, it would go precisely where he wished.

The stream of *direction* he bound into the render put it on a collision course for the very orange Raba had smacked his head against. The sphere punched a hole through it, bursting pulp and juice and shattered rinds in all directions, but especially into Mara's face.

Mara was not quite so precise, but she was by far Saya's best concentrator. Mara could ignore a trumpet in her ear, a feather tickling her feet, and an odor of raw sewage and bind her streams with ease. So rendering through the sticky pulp on her face was no problem at all.

She rendered a flash of bright light in Tashim's eyes, like a tiny sun in the yard. The light was so fierce it blinded Tashim for a moment. He shrieked and stumbled, tipping off the edge of the porch into the dirt. This elicited still more laughter from the other students.

The screen door burst open and Lili hurtled like a little brown-haired projectile onto the porch. "What is happening?! What did I miss?!" She held a little cup in one hand, sloshing more than half the water out of it.

"Lili!" Saya shouted. "You are spilling your water again."

Lili froze. She panicked and tried to lift the cup to her lips to chug it all down in one gulp, but the cup suddenly cracked under the grip of her fingertips. Her eyes went wide and the cup split in half, water splashing across her shirt. Her hands went to her hips and her brow narrowed. "Qudra!"

Saya heard a chuckle. Qudra had a habit of increasing the amount of stress on an object to the very point of breaking and then watching his victim shatter that thing with the lightest of touches.

That is another new cup we need now. "Jaytat, Qudra!" Saya tried to make her voice angry. She thought she did a pitiable job of it, but it must have worked. She heard Qudra gasp and then his feet trotting away to hide behind the shed.

Noqer shook his head and laughed, wandering back into the house.

Every day that goes by he tries to act older and older.

Somewhere in the yard Lili began to cry. Saya put her head in her hands, kneading the stress out of her eyes.

"You have to talk to him," Adrani said over her shoulder.

Saya was startled yet again. "Aya Jaytat, what now?"

"Noqer," Adrani said, fiddling with her braid, her sharpened gemstone eyes gazing out at the row of cedars.

"About what?"

"He is misbehaving."

Saya chuckled. "After this chaotic display I doubt he could do much worse."

"I catch him spying on me when I bathe."

Saya stiffened to ice. "He is of an age where he thinks about girls. The glance of a boy is what it is. Boys' eyes wander."

"I know you want to believe it is only just that. I want to believe it, too. But it felt strange, uncomfortable. The way he watches makes me feel...afraid."

Saya turned to look in her eyes. "You are worried."

"I said I think you should talk with him."

"He would be too embarrassed."

"Are you not my teacher? Are you not the woman who taught me not to run from my responsibilities just because they are difficult?"

"The curse of all good teachers," Saya said. "They teach so well their students teach it back at them."

Adrani cracked a smile. "Talk with him. He will listen to you. You know he will. He does not listen to me. Better to do it now before he does something else."

"You are right. I will. And soon." She was already dreading the awkwardness of it. But if one of her students felt afraid at home, that was too much. No one should ever be made to feel unsafe here.

Oh, Noqer. I remember when you were just a skinny little street boy. Now I must already talk to you about the comings and goings of being a man. She was not looking forward to it.

Saya whistled out a breath and lifted herself off the bench when she heard the grate squeal and groan and slide off to one side. It was only Radir. He hoisted himself out of the drain.

Holy Juna, please let him not have been followed.

Radir's sun-kissed face was a dour mask this day, eyes a piercing blue, his expression as sour as a squeeze of lemon. Even his familiar little smirk was gone.

Saya rose and walked to him, barefooted across the dirt and dry leaves, kicking off those that stuck to her toes. "What have you to tell, sweet Radir?"

He looked at her contemplatively. He did not speak but held out his hand, something in his fingers. Saya reached out her own hand. Radir dropped seven small copper coins into her palm.

She frowned. "This is all?"

He shrugged with his eyebrows alone. "Many nervous people on the streets."

Saya looked defeated. She rolled the coins around in her hand, and rolled her tongue around in her mouth. Her feet sank into the ground. She felt her whole body pulled down into the earth and crushed beneath the fear and the shame. The shame of failure. The shame of losing so much of their coin to Sevastin Karda's cruel whim. The fear of not having enough to pay the fee.

If only I hadn't gone to watch the children in the Old King's Square that day.

"That makes ten days in a row of poor takes."

"Those damned Glassdogs scare more than those like us. They have the thieves and gangs of every warren looking over their shoulders and jumping at their own shadows."

Saya's shoulders dropped. She bit her lip and looked away. "I am worried."

"We still have enough to eat," he said. "Raba stole a whole sack of apples two days past."

"Yet our stores are almost gone," she said. "And the pond has less and less fish." She looked him in his ice-blue eyes again. She hid her fear well from her students, put a mask over it the way the Priests wore gold to mask their cruelty, but Radir was old enough that she could be honest with him about it. "I have not paid Jacobas for the month. He is coming soon."

"Do we have enough?" Radir asked

She shook her head. "Close, but even with what was left of the coin Timma and Beni brought us we are short, and nothing left to buy bread or olive oil."

"You could work a trade with him," Radir suggested. "You have convinced him to grant an extension in the past."

Saya glared at him. "You say that as if it is easy for me to give."

"Is it not?" he asked. Radir was cold and hard inside sometimes.

She looked down at the coins in her hand. "No, it is not. I do it for the children. I do it for you. I do it because I must."

"I could burn him," Radir suggested matter-of-factly. "He should not make you do that. He should not make us pay at all. He doesn't own these walls."

"It is his street," Saya said. "Whatever he asks we have to pay. Killing him would change nothing. The warren-boss would only give the neighborhood to another enforcer...one who may be even more unkind. One word from him would bring the warren-boss, and our peaceful home would be no more."

"Someday I will kill the warren-boss," Radir said. "And you and all of us will live here for free, and owe nothing to no one."

"Someday," Saya agreed. "Not today."

Radir smiled. "No matter how bad today is, there is always a chance tomorrow will be better."

"And the good thing about tomorrows is that there always is one." She half-smiled, but it hurt. "Though for now it is still today, and today we need more coin."

"When is he coming?" Radir asked. "Maybe I can take Tashim and Qudra back out on another run. We have done daytime runs before. The merchant street by the Moneychanger is always an ocean of rich purses."

"Too late," Saya said, ducking beneath an errant birch bark projectile from Aafi practicing across the yard. She shot him a warning glance, and he froze, but then she smiled, and so did he.

Just then Saya heard echoes from down in the drain, careless splashing footsteps.

Saya paled. She swallowed her heart, choked, went numb.

He was here.

He was already here.

It was too early in the day. She was not ready to do this. She was not ready to endure Jacobas. She clapped her hands five times signaling to her students to cease everything they had been working on and be silent.

Saya waited for it. She knew it would come. The footsteps stopped. She held her breath.

Jacobas pounded incoherently on the grate from below. He pushed it up an inch or two several times letting it clang back down with the sharp biting sound, like a baby first discovering a new plaything. Radir lifted the grate, sliding it aside.

Jacobas hauled himself irreverently out into the courtyard. He dusted off his crimson wool tunic, and slapped the mud off his leggings. He scowled. "I should charge you a double fee for making me wander through that stinking darkness."

Every word from his mouth was like someone splashing a ladle of oil on her face. He radiated disgust.

"Why are you here?" Saya asked.

Jacobas snarled at her, his lower lip like a fat glistening worm. "Where is your payment? The month ended three days ago."

"Radir," Saya said. "Please bring the cup."

Radir stalked across the courtyard and disappeared into the main house. He returned with the cup, a tiny iron pot missing its handle, the coins within jingling as he walked.

Jacobas snatched it up like an old miser, overturned it, dumping its contents into his hand. He moved the coins around in his palm with his thumb, twirling the cup in the air with his other hand.

Please let it be enough. Please.

He counted every coin twice, then looked up at her accusingly. "You are short again," he said, his lips spilling into a grin. "And it is going to cost you."

"How much?" Saya asked.

His smile vanished. "Twenty silvers...plus what you are short...plus next month's fee by the time the moons dance."

Saya's eyes went wide. "That is only twenty days from now."

"It is what it is," he spat. "You are late. You deserve a penalty."

"We cannot get so much in so short a time."

"You will if you want to keep living here," Jacobas said, licking a blob of drool from the scruff on his chin. "They never notice that these walls have no door. Do you know why? Because I make it so. I keep the warren-boss from finding out about your little kingdom. I could always tell him what you are truly up to."

Saya's blood went cold. *No, please. Don't tell.*

He judged her thoughts by her expression. "I did not think you would."

Saya shuddered. She forced a smile to conceal it.

His own smile curdled hers. "Once more for the sake of old times? You used to not think so poorly of me."

She narrowed her eyes. "You and I are not together anymore."

"Do you think you are being treated unfairly? Because I doubt any of the other warrenborn would give you the deal I do. The Priests would pay quite the coin to learn about this place. I wager I could sell the information to them for double what you pay me in a year...but I won't. Not as long as you remain a gracious hostess when I visit."

She closed her eyes and took a long breath to steel herself. She would do what she must for the children. Whatever it took. She was not a warrior. She could not even make a shield to protect the smallest of her students.

She built for herself systems that would protect them for her. She built them a secret place of safety. She designed it to have high walls and no doors or windows. She built a secret space, with a secret entrance. She set up networks of different routes back, with dozens of cleaning stations in abandoned places all across the city. She did not have physical strength, but she had her own forethought, her preparation, her determination.

Everything was a small price compared to the lives of her beloved children. She would use whatever Holy Juna gave her to see her will done. She had lost so many people already. She could not lose another.

"We have a deal then?" he asked. "I would hate to have to report you. It would not go well for the children."

Saya nodded. She tried to wish the nausea away. She waved Radir away as Jacobas slid the coins into one filthy pocket. "Keep them going. Keep them training. Keep them out there in the yard." She stared hard at him. "Do not let them come over there to look for me. Please."

Radir must have noticed the pain in her face. He puffed out his lip and stood straight. "I won't."

"Remember what Khersas used to say?"

"*Leave now. Come back stronger. Fight when you can win.*"

She nodded and smiled half-heartedly.

She led Jacobas by the hand around the side of the main house, behind the poplar tree, careful to walk him well around the areas where the children had been practising their magick, so that not even a whisper of afterglow would make it onto his clothes. Beyond the poplar sat a narrow strip of land between the house and the inner edge of one high brick wall where they stored old ropes, nails, and mortar clay. The house had no windows here.

This place was worth whatever she had to do to keep it. Her money, her dignity, her life. She would give it all. She prayed what little it was worth would be enough.

In her heart she knew that one day, she would come back stronger, she would fight and win, and she would never have to give him anything ever again.

We will go far away from here someday.

One of these tomorrows will lead us to a better life.

As long as the tomorrows keep coming, one of them will be that day.

And the good thing about tomorrows is that there always is one.

6

Glassdog

"I AM SO AFRAID," she said.

"To live in Kasaban is to live with fear," Terak said. "Always."

"I know," Saya said.

He pushed the stack of silver coins across the table to her. The wind kicked up outside just then, whistling hard at the corners of his window shutters, jarring loose a fog of white dust. "This I can loan. Only."

"I understand. Thank you. It means everything to me. We will have more in twenty sunrises, when the caravan we sell to comes in."

"You tell this story three times, yes," he said, crossing his fingers, elbows on the table across from her, molten light from his lamp making a golden circle of the space between them.

"I talk too much," she said.

"More like you are convincing yourself to take this, than me to give it," he said. "Seems so."

She could not deny how right he was. She hated holding out her hand to a friend for something she had not earned. It made a tight knot of her gut, a pin stabbing her heart, a sinking fire in her throat. To borrow was to aggrieve. "My parents taught me to always take care of my needs myself."

"Kasaban is not this way."

"Walk the sands alone and the sun shall bleach your bones. Walk the sands together and you'll have water forever."

"Is good proverb."

"Written by someone who did not have fifteen mouths to feed."

He shrugged at her.

"Any ideas?" she asked.

"Picking of pockets?"

She chuckled. "My invisibility is not perfect. It bends and warps. The eye can see it. It is most effective in darkness, or disturbed light, like sunshine through leaves. The sun on the clouds is so bright it washes out afterglow, but my magick itself would be seen."

"Night?"

"My magick would blend better, but the afterglow would be so noticeable. Besides, that is when they let out the most Glassdogs at once."

"Pickpockets make fortune on sunny day. Why not steal from the thieves?"

"Terak, that is just..."

"Who they ask for help?"

"Magick makes glittering light when it forms, even little magick. The Priests have Glassdogs. They are always watching." She mimicked goggles with her fingers and held them up to her eyes.

He shrugged. "I think this much."

"Thank you, Terak. I am sure we will think of something. We will find a way." But when she said it, she felt the same way she did when she was lying.

He smiled at her from the darkness and waved.

She opened the door and everything turned to light. She closed the door and looked up at the sky. Clouds today, a patchwork quilt of white tufts over blue, one fat one sitting over the sun. It was a cool summer day for Kasaban. Cool enough that if she stood in the shade she could last minutes before being overwhelmed with sweat.

She turned to head home, skirting around the poormarkets. She would rather not have to see all the things she could not afford this day. She did not even have enough to purchase a calpas from Xarla.

So she went for a stroll down the alley where the old gods lived, walking past their outlines, chalk in many layers, redrawn again and again, a thousand layers deep after the test of wind and rain and sun—the three emissaries of time. She listened to each of the effigies cry out from the ages, raging tears against the cascade of time.

She held out one finger and touched each of the images, skipping her feet, trying, as she always did, to let her heart be free for the length of this one narrow alley. But this time the freedom did not come, only fear. The fear of losing her home, the safe place she built, the secret paths she mapped out, the cleaning rooms she stocked, everything she had done all her life to build the protection that her body and her magick could not achieve on their own.

I have worked too hard to lose what I have.

The alley spat her out into a heavy crowd on one of the widest streets in Kasaban. Her feet crashed into a dust mountain, great white plumes flaring into the air at every kick of her feet.

A wealthy man felt a glob of it splash his ankle and he looked down on her like she was refuse. He made a sour face and went on. The dunemakers chastised her nonetheless. They had their protocols, after all. The dust belonged in the gutters, and they slapped and beat at her shins and ankles with their enormous bristly brooms, swiping her until she was safely back on the outer edge, up against the wall where the poor and inconsequential belonged.

She ignored their jeers, and joined the crowd, one drop of water into a river. She pulled her hood up, to keep the blistering sun off her neck, and to keep her face from the eyes of any watchers.

She thought of what Terak had said. *Why not steal from the thieves?* Was it even possible?

She became a bobbing head in the crowd, but unlike the rest, she was studying everyone, watching for the swift darting movements of pickpockets. She saw three before she even reached the compound of the Moneychanger, including one just outside the black iron gate. None of them dared rob the people in line though. If they were caught the people in line would become a mob and lynching was not out of the question.

She kept going to the edge of the city, then back again. Each time she saw one more. There must have been dozens out at a time. So many pockets turned from jingling to whispering.

The thieves do make off with much.

Then she remembered that she and her students *were* thieves. Just because they only thieved to supplement their income did not absolve them from those thefts.

But even using magick, all her students together could never pull off as many thefts as just one of these young boys, in so short a span. Runts with half sandals and matted hair carved their way through the crowds with fingers as precise as a surgeon's tools. They swarmed the bustling streets and the crush at every market stall.

She tried to track them, follow one from place to place, but they were so small and so fast they vanished from sight every other step. And they did it all without magick.

Saya had been using her magick for so long she was not sure she knew how to be stealthy without it. Herein lay the problem. Every one of her students had been building their skills for so long that they wanted to use their powers to solve every problem, answer every question. And then they forgot how to do without it. Or they never learned how. Magick became their reflex action. That could be a problem with so many men with the lens looking about.

After her fifth circuit, her eyes began to glaze over. She could not track any of the little thieves long enough to see where they went with their earnings or glimpse their masters. The pickpockets began to phase out of her mind, blending in with the energy of the street, merging into the crowd the way an extra footstep would.

She was about to diverge and head home, but for one thing that caught her eye. A small boy, smaller than all the rest, crept up behind a tall man in wealthy white silks. The boy seemed nervous, not as experienced as the others. She found herself hoping, even praying, that he would succeed, that he would escape with coin in hand. She needed him to.

He reached one hand deftly into the coinpurse swaying from a golden belt. But he did not realize the man kept two swift bodyguards, each dressed nearly as finely as he, in white linen robes, belts of black leather twine, long knives in Borean buffalo hide sheaths.

When his fingers were halfway into the purse, one of the bodyguards reached out and swatted his hand. The boy turned to look, terrified. The bodyguard grabbed him by the collar, lifting him off the ground. The other slipped a knife free, pulling back to stab. The boy shrieked.

Saya froze. Her stomach caught in her throat. Her hand reached out on its own, and before she could blink, before she even realized she had dipped into the source, she rendered magick.

The boy disappeared, wreathed in a lightbending bubble, invisible. The hand holding him vanished with him. The bodyguard panicked and dropped the boy. Saya had not tethered the bubble to him, so it remained floating in the air. The boy fell out the bottom of the bubble and scurried away, before the bubble winked out, leaving a hiss of silver steam and a waft of glittering gas, floating on the air like flame.

The people around it gasped and backed away. The two bodyguards and their patron circled it, pointing at it, too afraid to touch it, the color spilling through the air. A crowd formed about them.

Saya stared at them.

Holy Juna, what have I done?

She watched the crowd. No one looked at her. No one noticed her. She was alone. She was safe.

No one knows.

Holy Juna, thank you for the blessing of your light.

The afterglow was small and already faded to the naked eye. Soon enough it would fade to less than what even the lens of a Glasseye could see.

She curled her fingers into fists, crossed her arms and tucked them into either side of her stomach. She could not risk the afterglow on her hands coming in contact with anything.

Until it faded from her palms and fingertips, it would rub off onto anything, and if spotted could be used to track her location. Anything she touched and left behind could become a beacon, alerting the Ministry Glasseyes to where she was.

And the worst of it was she herself could not even see whether it had faded or not. The side-effect of her magick was invisible even to her. But not to those who had the lenses of the Glasseyes. She only knew how long it took to clean her hands with the proper amount of water, ranum crystal salts, and obsidian sand.

I have to get to one of our safe havens. I have to wash my hands, change my clothes just to be safe.

She was planning carefully, thinking clearly, a plan formulated. She had prepared for this and done it many times. Each of the safe havens she had set up not only afforded quiet places to hide and wait out afterglow, and to make certain she was not followed before returning home, but they also had changes of clothing, washbasins, and even some special soaps. She had stocked them and always kept them up. She was careful.

Until she saw him.

Sevastin Karda, in a white robe and gold mask, walked nonchalantly down the cross street, flanked by two Priests dressed as he was. A city governor was forced to walk backwards ahead of him in order to converse, trying not to trip and fall while discussing city matters.

No, not him.

As they were walking, suddenly Karda stopped, turned, and looked directly at her. He must have been thirty paces away, with dozens of pedestrians and the canopy of three merchant stalls between them, but it felt so clearly that he was looking at her. It was like a knife to the heart. Her legs melted and she nearly fell down.

He blessedly turned back to the city governor and continued walking.

Saya turned and ran, taking corners at a run, cutting through a narrow alley with shallow-walled patios full of children, and mothers cooking in unwieldy ceramic pots.

The fear overrode all. She did not think. She careened through a lonely arched path between two white stone tenements, and rounded a corner.

She crashed headlong into a man. Her head smacked against his chest, sending her stumbling back. She barely pulled her arms up in time to keep from rubbing the invisible stains of her magick from her hands onto his coat.

His eyes peered out like lizard moons from beneath two perfect circles of opaque crystal, goggles strapped over his eyes with squeaky-tight brown leather as worn and sunbaked as his coat.

The Glassdog tilted his head down so slowly to look at her, lips peeled back, mouth baring teeth, drool leaking down his chin. His eyes seemed enormous through the lenses, as if they were reaching out from his face and touching her. When they fell upon her hands, her belly and chest where she had wiped them, those eyes grew even larger, opening like roaring mouths.

He saw the afterglow.

She could not tell if he was soaring into the sky above her, or if she was sinking into the earth at his feet. Her heart raced, thunderous and violent, her breaths choked, her thoughts unspooling, her soul evaporating.

His eyes screamed at her.

She reached out and slapped him with the back of her hand. The blow sent a burst of pain across her wrist, showering her fingers with tingling fire. His face turned against the blow, the goggles going askew.

Saya turned and ran, robes swirling in the air about her.

Her feet felt leadened, her legs trudging against a lake of mud. But when she looked down it was only flat earth and air. She did not look back, but she felt always that he was breathing against her neck the whole time.

She had not left any afterglow on him, nor could she have sensitized anything else. He had not seen the render she had made. He only knew what she looked like, and that she had afterglow on her. He could not track her with it. Not yet. All she needed to do was escape him. Get away from his eyes without touching anything else he would be able to find. He could not track her once she was out of his sight. That was all.

She could not hope to fight him with her hands, and she most certainly could not use her magick against him. If she did, he could stop chasing her and simply track her for hours afterward, leading a coterie of Priests to her at home.

Run. Hide. Wait. Survive.

She took turns at random, hoping to lose him, hoping he would tire or lose interest. She paused in the markets, and turned to look back only once. He was right there with her, lips tight around a lunatic smile, gnarled hand reaching out at her collar, chipped and cracked fingernails wanting to close around her throat.

She ducked behind the merchant carts, spun past stunned people, crawled beneath tables, and hurtled around corners. Sun beating down on her skin, her heart beating back against it from within. Her lungs burned, her breaths smoked, her blood seared, threatening to turn her flesh into flame. Her legs raced the wind, pushing her along so fast the dust stood still in the air around her. Her ears held no sounds but for her panicked breathing and the footsteps of the man behind her.

Her mind screamed, her thoughts hopeless, thinking of the children, wondering who would take care of them after she was gone, wondering how she could kill herself rather than be captured and face the prospect of turning her students in under the heinous torture implements of the Inquisitors.

The Glassdog never slowed. Every person she ducked past, or pulled into the way, was knocked carelessly aside by him. Young or old, wealthy or poor, none would stand between the Glassdog and his prey. No one dared.

Every step she could gain was a boon. She ducked down alleys, ran along aqueducts, crossed irrigation channels, and wound as much of her trail through the tightest passages, the tallest buildings, so that not only could she escape him, but she would not risk any of his brothers seeing and joining in the chase.

Please, Holy Juna, let no one witness my passage.

She begged her feet to keep going, pleaded with her lungs to keep drawing breath, and prayed that her heart not give out under the baking sun.

My children need me. Please don't let me die.

She gained another seven paces when she threw herself between the wheels of the Moneychanger wagon, rolling out between the spears of its bodyguards. The Glassdog was caught up by their alarm, slowing him a precious few moments.

She gained another three paces when she turned herself sideways and slid between the solid front of the Light Procession celebrating Holy Juna. The Glassdog shouted, crashing headlong into them, having to shove his way through them, like swimming against a savage current.

She gained another five when she cut through the back rooms of an ice den, forcing him to check its every corner before following her into the alley behind.

She made her way back to a safehouse she had made in the basement beneath the abandoned first floor of a triple-story building split between two families. If she could only put enough distance between herself and the man chasing her, she could drop to her knees, crawl through the plants, push open the shutter, and squeeze herself in to hide.

She led him round in the same circles, gaining a step or two each time, until he was always just out of sight before she took each corner. She could hear his steps. She did not have time to turn back and look.

She needed every second.

If she could only make it to the first safehouse, she could clean herself and slip back into the anonymous crowds. There was a basin, a large drum of water stopped with cork, and a change of clothes. Everything she needed.

She shoved her way through a gate, tore her robes wide climbing over a wall, and bloodied her knees crawling through an irrigation duct for the Old King's Square. Her foot twisted into a cramp, her throat burned like she had swallowed salt. But she finally purchased enough space with her pain and determination.

She reached the high back wall of the house and threw herself up, clutching the top with her hand and forearms. Hooked her arms over. Swung her legs up. Scraped her knees bloody on the edge. She rolled herself over the top, but was too rushed, taking breaths too fast, fingers slipping, legs tumbling over, dragging the rest of her with them.

She crashed to the ground, and managed to land feet-first, but sprained both ankles, collapsing her onto her side. She dragged herself on hands and knees over the dry dirt, through the wall of desert scrub, thornbrush tearing at her shoulders and hips, ducking her head, crawling blindly to keep the spines away from her face.

At last she was through, the house inches away, the basement shuttered window just ahead, where the wall met the ground.

She glanced over her shoulder, saw nothing, heard nothing. She pulled the small shutter aside and slid through head-first, her robes tearing at the shoulder and ripping all the way down one arm. She kicked her way through, her hands walking her down the inside wall. She dropped. Her hands absorbed some of the landing, but her head took much more, pain shining so bright she could not see, waves of throbbing spasms running down her neck.

She rolled flat on her back, and looked up at the tiny window. Her breaths sounded so loud she was certain he could have heard her miles away. She stared at the window. Her mind kept imagining him coming through, so vividly each time she thought it was real, that he was there, but he never came in.

Get up.

Get up!

She rolled over and crawled through a short tunnel Khersas had carved through the wall to a storeroom unused by any of the current tenants, its old door long since bricked over.

Within she saw the basin, the container of water, and the jar of ranum crystal soap. She unstoppered the water and poured it into the basin, running her hands all through it, splashing it on her face. She scrubbed her hands and arms relentlessly with the soap, all the way up to the elbows. Rendering magick always seemed to leave afterglow clinging to her hands. She then scrubbed at her face. She peeled herself out of her robes and left them submerged.

She lit rosewood in a tiny stone censer, and let the smoke wash over her skin. She lay flat on her back, panting, heart still racing as if she was running at full speed. She found a clean robe, one Khersas had bought for her with hard-earned money years ago, waiting here all this time for her, for a moment just like this. She pulled it on without standing up, her body refusing to be upright. She slid arms through sleeves and pulled her head through, squirming the rest of the way into it, cinching it at the waist with a soft rope belt.

She reached over to douse the incense when she heard the shutters kicked open. Her eyes filled with water so fast she went blind. Her fingers refused to pick anything up, her legs refused to run. She heard him moving through the tunnel.

She realized it then. In her panic to escape, she had used her hands to pull herself over the wall, to scramble through the bushes, to pull open the shutters. She must have left a stain of afterglow everywhere her fingers touched. Invisible to her. Invisible to everyone. Only able to be seen by someone looking through those crystal lenses, the ones pinned to his eyes by those goggles.

She ran to the wall and picked up the stoneware basin, dumping out the water. The Glassdog burst out of the tunnel, quickly rising. She brought the basin down over his head, cracking it in two. He fell beneath it, one hand grabbing her and dragging her down atop him. She brought both pieces of the basin down over him again, hitting his skull, stunning him, rolling off and crawling back out of the tunnel into the basement.

He was already up, coming after her. She knew she had to stop him now, not just escape him. Even if she shook him from her tail, he could lead others to the stains of afterglow she had left on the wall and the shutters. He could lead the Priests to her.

When she emerged into the basement she scanned it for something to hit him with, tie him up, block the exit. Just long enough for the afterglow she left behind to fade enough that no one could track her with it. Just then she saw the face of Radir looking at her through the shutters.

"Radir," she gasped.

He held out a hand to her. "Come."

"He is..." Her breaths interrupted her speech. "There is..."

"I know." He took her hand and heaved her through.

She sat on the hot dirt, looking through the basement window, seeing the Glassdog's hands coming back out of the tunnel. "Radir!"

Radir did not answer her. Instead, he dipped into the source, flooding himself with the Slipstream. He found his streams, the ones that could alter the amount of heat, the ones that could rewrite the story of the universe with one tiny change. He brought those streams together in his mind and bound them.

"We can't," she said. "The afterglow."

"They will not see it," he said.

"They will track it."

"They will not track it."

"If you render something within that room, it will leave vapors, glowing on every surface they touch. It will be all over that room."

He turned to look at her. "There will not be any room after this."

She saw the Glassdog's head come through the tunnel, tilting up, looking across the basement, meeting her eyes through the window. "What are you...?"

Radir was frighteningly calm. "Everything that exists has a temperature at which it will become flame. This basement and all its furnishings and decorations are made of wood."

Saya watched as Radir rendered his change into reality. The temperature within the basement skyrocketed, the air bending and waving, shimmering black and pink. And then, in a flash of light, the entire room erupted at once into flame. The air within became a roaring inferno. The

Glassdog screamed for barely a second before his clothes and flesh became the wick of a candle. He did not simply catch fire, he *became* fire, his scream ending in a gust of steam from within him.

Radir pulled Saya away, her eyes locked on that basement. The flames grew, rising up, taking the upper levels with it, until the entire building was engulfed in an inferno, red-orange flame licking the sky, roaring as it consumed everything.

Seven people scrambled out of it, leaping off balconies and racing down stairs. The tenants. Saya covered her mouth with her hands.

What have we done?

She cried into her palms.

We have destroyed their homes.

The flames spread so quickly, that they had no time to save anything they owned. They had simply become homeless and penniless. Their lives had been destroyed.

"Radir," she whispered.

"I wish it did not have to be this way."

"They are families, Radir. Little children."

He shrugged. "At the end of the day they are all only normals."

Only normals. The callousness of his words had been bought with years of fear and sorrow crushing him, but still it shocked her. It sounded so much like the way everyone else spoke about magi, about their kind.

Radir departed, heading back to the street to see if any Glasseyes or Glassdogs had seen the afterglow of her invisible bubble.

Saya made herself watch the crying children and the mothers and fathers falling to their knees in despair, embracing each other against the agony of their murdered futures. She made herself watch what she and Radir had done just as she made herself watch what the Priests did to her kind.

Radir was right; there was no way to see his afterglow through the flames. They ate the afterglow as they ate the dreams of those families.

At last, Radir returned. "They are not searching the street, not talking to witnesses. They have found nothing of what you did back there. They would have been studying the area. We are safe."

Saya wept at the flames of the dying homes. "Are we?"

"We should go," he said.

She did not argue. She knew he was right.

But for the first time she felt wrong.

7

Exarch

SEVASTIN KARDA KNELT UPON the remembrance spikes, a coarse plum-colored veritas cloak draped over him like folds of stretched skin. The pain in his knees had dulled, a slick of blood pooling under each, warming him. He welcomed the blood and the pain. In the search for ultimate truth, even one's own flesh was a lie. He whispered a prayer and let the pain remind him of the joy of truth. For there was no greater path to truth than pain.

The Holy Autarch loomed over him, marble limbs smooth as fresh organelles, thickly muscled and reverent, gazing upon him with enormous lidless eyes. Those eyes could see through his skin to the truth at his deepest core. Those eyes could see his innermost desire to exalt the Lord of Truth who was the Lord of Magick who was the Master of the Realm of the White Light of Possibility. The Holy Autarch knew, and so the Lord of Truth knew, that there was no heart more devoted to bringing about the Advent, thereby ensuring His return to bathe the world in his purifying incandescence.

By the second hour, the blood from his knees had thickened and crisped, but the pain never fully subsided.

The door opened behind him. He had been in silence for so long he had forgotten where he was, and who was coming to visit him. It all came back in a rush of glandular terror, slicking the rotten lie of his flesh with molten sweat.

Above him stood the only three men who held power over him for over a hundred leagues in any direction—Gethilric, the Exarch of Masaba, Kraab, the Judge of Mekrash Valley, and Caeron, Holy Marshall of the Golden Gate. All of them had shed their individual vestments for the purple robes of the gorgeous decay, to remind themselves of the impurity of their own blood, and the rot of their own bodies.

The three hovered over him, carrion birds silently negotiating their bites. They did not wear the golden masks. They were not a part of the crusade, so their faces were bare. Though each resembled his function.

Caeron was square of jaw and round of head, fingers squeezing as if he was crushing the bones of the unholy in his fists. Kraab looked down a scythe of a nose, one subtle bow away from slicing Karda's head from his body. And Gethelric, of course, had the bemused smile of one who spent quiet moments kissing his gold, and making love to cheers from crowds of the devout at every midday prayer.

Sevastin Karda was guilty of envy.

He loved the Lord of Truth more than Gethelric, and one day would see the Exarch bend to kiss his feet, the way they made Holy Juna kiss the feet of the Lord of Truth.

"Prelate Karda," Gethelric said, bemused.

Karda did not appreciate such an expression in a place of holiness. "Exarch."

"How pleased I was to hear of your elevation from Master Adept," Gethelric said, in a tone much reminiscent of someone who means the opposite of what they say.

Karda kept his head bowed. "It is my only pleasure to serve the Lord of Truth in whatever role he deems for me."

"You have been captain of the crusade in Mekrash Valley for a good long while," Gethelric said.

"Many demons in that desert, Exarch," Karda said.

They all think me beneath them. They will wake up one day to find they are mistaken.

"Your progress has drawn many an eye back in Almar," Gethelric said. "Madinas, Nabena, Rhodas, all liberated from the clutches of the unholy."

"I do only what the Lord of Truth expects of me, Exarch."

"Your name is often spoken of favorably in the most powerful circles."

Karda maintained his bow to hide his delirious smile. "I am pleased my devotion to the mission of the Lord of Truth has been noticed."

"The Autarch is considering creating a new Exarchate," Gethelric said.

Karda could not help but lift his head to look at them. "Only one step away from the Autarch himself."

"Centered in Kasaban," Gethelric said.

"My city," Karda said.

"Some names have been floated," Gethelric said. "But the will of the Ministry council seems bent on celebrating the creation of this new position by giving it to a hero of the faith."

"Someone who can purify the unclean," Caeron said. "And purge the land of abomination."

It is to be me. It must be. I am the one. I will make Kasaban a jewel in the crown of our Autarch. That is why they loathe to say it.

"Of course, there is one small matter," Judge Kraab said. The fact that he was the one chosen to say it meant it was to be the worst sort of news.

Karda attempted to shrug it off. "Only one?"

Kraab's leech of a mouth wiggled into a smile. "It would be unseemly to create such an exalted position when the purity of the city that is to be its seat remains in question."

Karda choked back the urge to leap to his feet, take Kraab's neck with both hands and squeeze until he vomited his last breath past his bloated tongue. "The city of Kasaban is pacified."

"That is not the rumor floating around our holy cathedral in Almar, Prelate Karda," the Judge said.

If he had been leaning but a span closer, Sevastin Karda would have bitten open the Judge's throat and let his blood splash the exalted statue's feet. "Rumors are only that."

"Rumors have a power of their own," Gethelric said. "They can shape perception."

"They speak of a Teacher," Judge Kraab said. "Hiding right under your nose."

Karda bit his tongue to keep from screaming in rage at the mention. "A simple demon, nothing more. A rogue hiding in shadows. The Teacher is powerless."

"The way it is spoken of in Almar is that the masses whisper prayers to the Teacher whenever your back is turned." Kraab always seemed to enjoy twisting the knife.

"Perhaps the ears would ring happier if the rumors were instead of the burning of the Teacher and the total purification of the city," Caeron said, in a manner indicating it was far from a suggestion.

"The streets of Kasaban are clear," Karda assured them. "I have brought in Glassdogs from the holy city."

Exarch Gethelric smiled. "If your little problems in the shadows can be tidied up, I see little reason why a ceremony for the coronation of a new Exarch could not be scheduled before Midwinter's Day."

Karda bowed low so that none of them could see him licking his lips.

All three exited the temple, but Gethelric lingered. "The Autarch is watching, Prelate Karda. Do not fail him."

"Never, Sacred Exarch."

Sevastin Karda knelt alone, feeling the spikes bite anew into the raw flesh of his knees. The pain reminded him of his goal.

The Teacher.

I shall cast the unholy into the fires. I shall make their skin crackle in the flames of their purification. The lie of their flesh will be freed in screams and flame, and left in its true ashen form.

8

A City Of Murdered Gods

STANDING OVER THE PIT, looking down at the pieces of broken gods, she felt the vastness of her people's loss.

Every statue, whether of marble or basalt, lapis or porphyry, had been snapped apart and crumbled, the remnant chunks of stone tumbled into a vacant quarry on the outskirts of the city. Kasaban would know no gods but those the Priests decided.

She saw more than a few people crawling among the dangerous jumble of stone blocks, braving the treacherous peaks, crevasses and defiles, risking death to look for pieces of their deities.

Sometimes a chunk of stone with an arm or part of a face would be found. They would mark them in secret, a way only their sect would recognize, so that others could make a pilgrimage across the field of sacred wreckage.

Kasaban had once been free to all people, to all religions and all cultures, a place where people of every heritage and background could come together and *belong*. A hundred religions gathered from all over the world in harmony only to be wiped out by the hundred-and-first.

The Ministry.

The Priests really do take everything.

Saya turned away from the haphazard shards of religion, leaving the detritus of faith to those who still felt comfort clinging to it.

At least she still had Holy Juna.

Her temples remained.

Expanded even.

She entered the first one she saw, a small door between two enormous pillars. Within was a room of blue walls, an eternal midnight, benches lining either side of a long golden tongue of a rug. Incense of rose wafted within and three women were already inside, kneeling, whispering, crying.

The shrine at the far end had once been a smooth statue of Juna kneeling down so that one could pray by touching foreheads with her. Now though, it had been replaced with the pale marble likeness of a regal Priest standing tall in robes of white with disdainful empty eyes, and the place where one put their forehead was now upon his foot.

The Priests attempted to sell a version of Holy Juna that was weak, subservient, obsequious. It was a juvenile misunderstanding of her nature. For the sacred texts told of a Juna who was quite active, even aggressive, in dedication to her people. She was a fighter. But she fought to protect and preserve, not for power or conquest.

The Priests were more than happy to have a regional god who prized submission. But Juna was a submission of the self to the help of others. It was the Priests who corrupted her message and turned it into one that prepared the way for servitude to the oppressive overlords.

The temple-mistresses read the words drafted by the invaders, but they quietly kept the prayers and symbolic rituals that offered the true meaning of Holy Juna, the protection of family and devotion to each other as a community. That is what Saya prayed to every minute of every day of her life.

The elders once said that during the prehistoric wars of centuries, Holy Juna saved the people by turning herself into a light so bright she outshined the sun, hiding her faithful from the bloodletting demons, leaving no shadows and turning her enemies to dust.

Holy Juna was strong. I hope every day I can be as strong as she.

Saya whispered a quiet prayer and left.

She wound round the old pond, dried to half its size by too many long summers. She found some iron filaments half-buried in the mud and picked them up, rinsing them in what little muddy water remained.

These will make good hooks for Noqer to fish with. A little heat treatment from Radir to shape them and the boys could make them perfect.

She continued on her way, beginning her journey in the center of the street, but the further she went, the further she was pushed to the outside by the brooms of the dunemakers and the sharp elbows of the city governor's street soldiers until at last she was up against the walls kicking through white dust and sand up to her shins.

Where she belonged.

It was like a microcosm of her whole life, how she began so vibrant and proud, and was slowly shifted by fear and pain to the outside edges of her own world. Oh, how she hated the city that she used to love.

She had not meant to walk by the Excruciation stage. She arrived there quite unintended, her feet delivering her there without guidance from her mind.

She looked up at the vacant platform, wide pale stone, the color of ash. The empty horror of it staggered her—the stands still there where the bowls were placed to burn the faces, crusted with the oil of the dead; the weathered X-crosses where sometimes the women were nailed, spread-eagled, burned from their inner thighs up; the narrow stone tables where they burned the infants and toddlers.

Saya closed her eyes. Even now, in the baking silence of an empty Kasaban wind she could still hear the screams. All the screams. Every scream. Through all time, into the past, into the future. They rang out in her head like pealing bells.

Someday this place would have to be free of them. Someday. But how could she ever do anything for this place? She was living on the edge of a cliff every day of her life. Always one silver coin away from being cast out into the streets, always one careless moment away from being found out and burned alive.

I can barely make it through each day. I can barely keep a roof over our heads. I don't have time to solve the problems of the world.

She wished she could change Kasaban the way she wanted. But she knew it was only a pale dream.

Dreams are as worthless as a cup of salt when you are thirsty.

She followed the flow of people like a grain of sand tumbling on the wind. She watched them walk, watched them move. She blended with them. Became nameless, faceless.

She crossed the highmarket square, eyeing every table, jealous of the shade of their canopies, and envious of all the foods and wares she could not afford.

She saw a fishing pole that would have been perfect for Faloush, sandals for Lili, a cup for Qudra, candy for Aafi, a toy sword for Sotta, and a thousand other things that they could use, or could simply enjoy, to bring their lives a moment of happiness.

All of them cost too much money. With the looming deadline set by Jacobas, even a copper bit for one of the peppermints was too much to spare. Her mouth watered just long enough for the arid Kasaban sky to pull the water out of her, desiccating lips and tongue.

It was not fair.

She fumed at it, fumed at Holy Juna for letting these creatures with gold faces walk all over her people. She spat curses under her breath until the anger was spent, leaving her exhausted and unfulfilled. She apologized to Holy Juna. It was not like her to blaspheme, but she was stretched too far.

But then Holy Juna showed her something.

A little body, in a dirty tunic, bare feet, tiny hands, slowly floated up the back of one of the canopies where no one could see, just high enough to snag a blue citrus from the basket stored up there. There was no one watching them, the merchant obviously thinking them safely out of reach of even the tallest man.

But not safe from magi.

The little boy floated back down to the ground, landing cautiously, if unsteadily. Saya was astounded by his control. He gnashed his teeth into the blue citrus, devouring it as if he had not eaten in days.

When she saw the peddler turning his head in the boy's direction, Saya was jolted out of her delightful little fantasia, and shoved rudely back to the real world.

A world where they burned little boys like him alive. For being caught doing far less.

How can I help him without damning myself?

She looked all around herself. Saw no one nearby, no one looking at her. Judged the sun high enough in the sky. She flexed and constricted her fingers and rendered a tiny flat reflector near the ground, angled so that it would catch the light of the sun and stab a beam of it into the peddler's eyes.

The peddler raised a hand to his eye, shaking his head. The boy turned to see him there and darted around another cart full of spiced oils in slender glass bottles and escaped behind a white tent.

Saya glanced around once more, but no one noticed her render. The bright sunlight washed out the visibility of what tiny shimmer of pale afterglow accompanied her mirror into reality. It hovered at her ankles, slowly fading to invisibility. The light reflected at the peddler was real light, so it would not carry any afterglow with it.

She judged herself safe.

She tucked the hand she used to aid her focus for the render up into her sleeve, to remind herself not to touch anything else with it, lest she leave a stain of sensitized fluorescence upon anything that the Glassdogs might see.

She followed the little boy across the square, and into the walkway abutting an irrigation canal, between the water and a white wall lined with a legion of cedars. She did not attempt to hide her movement, nor did she try to get his attention. She let him discover her in his own time.

The boy noticed her and stopped, turned slowly until their eyes met.

"Don't be afraid," she said. "I am not here to hurt you."

"What do you want?" he asked. His voice was so small, he could not have been much older than Timma.

"You looked hungry," She said. She took a step toward him and knelt down. "I know of a place where you can find food and shelter. Where you would not have to wander for scraps. Where you could find shade in the day, and a hearth and roof to keep warm through the night. Where you may practice what you do safely."

"What I do?"

"Your special gift."

He grew defensive. "I have no gift."

"I do not know many boys your age who can walk on air."

Her words stunned him to silence. "What do you want?"

"To offer you a safe place."

"With you?"

She nodded. She held out a hand. "Come with me. I will take you to Saya's school."

His shoulders relaxed, and his eyes even grew a bit excited. "You know the teacher?"

"Teacher?"

"They all talk about the teacher," the boy said.

"Who does?"

"All of us," he said. "Every magick child who sleeps the streets and scrapes in the dirt to survive. We all know her. She is a defender."

Saya froze. Fear blazed through her like ravenous fire. She cupped a hand to her mouth, seeing her brother flash before her eyes. "Do not use that word."

"What word? Defender?"

"I am no defender."

His eyes widened. "Are you her?"

She stood up. "I have to go."

"Come back," he said. "I want to introduce you to everyone. They will not believe it."

I cannot protect anyone. I am not strong. I am weak. All I am good at doing is hiding. I make places to hide. That is all.

She turned to walk away, shivering in the heat.

That was when she saw the white robes.

Her breath snaked out of her mouth until her body felt so empty it could float away on the breeze. Her heart turned to paper, crumpling within her, aching so suddenly she held a fist to her chest.

"I told you she would lead us to one," the voice of a demon said. "I knew she would."

She could never forget that voice. Not if she lived a thousand years.

Sevastin Karda.

The White Death of Kasaban was here.

Saya froze. Her reflex was to render an invisible bubble about herself, and use it to escape. But she choked that instinct back down, like swallowing a heavy stone. She had already rendered. They had not found her trail yet, she knew, or the first words from Karda's mouth would have been whispered in her ear as he stood behind her, his hands wrapped about her throat.

No, they must not have found that trace. But if she dared try to save the child, they would be guaranteed to find it, killing her students as surely as if she pushed them in the fire with her own hands.

Ministry Priests meant Glasseyes, likely Glassdogs as well, waiting to record her magick, to capture her afterglow and track it. To follow her back to the children.

She could not allow that to happen.

Karda emerged with five other Priests across the canal, pale ghosts with gold faces, eyes eternal emotionless black holes, mouths open in infinite murder screams. With them came Glasseyes, men in linen coats down to their knees, leather cases slung over shoulders, bronze-framed crystal lenses in their hands. But at least they were on the far side of the canal. Too far to jump, no bridges nearby.

But they were Priests. Priests were magi-hunters, yes. But they were also magi themselves, ruthlessly policing their own kind with that very same magick. She had to prepare as if any one of them might be able to attack at a distance or deliver themselves across the water.

People gathered behind the Priests, leaning over railings and peeking around benches and columns.

On the near side were soldiers in white tunics and wide-brimmed hats with hoods over them. They held short spears, with truncheons tucked into black belts. And there was a Glassdog with them. His presence sent a shiver down her spine. She remembered the other one chasing her, running, crawling, then burning when the house took to flame around him.

She reached out for the little boy, but he pulled way from her. She tried to grab him but he ran at the soldiers.

No, boy! Come back!

"Go, Teacher! Go!" He rendered flat planes, perfect squares, ahead of him, and he bound into them a speed and direction, sending each of them sweeping across the ground, slamming into the soldiers one by one, shoving them back, knocking them down.

The Priests all turned to track his motion, even Karda.

Saya backed away, tripped, fell on her backside, and crawled backwards until she vanished into the trees. Once behind them she stood and ran parallel to the path the boy had taken, using the wall of cedars as a screen.

There must be something I can do to help him.

But there wasn't.

One of the Priests rendered squares of his own, stronger than those of the boy, closing them around him, bringing them together like the sides of a box. The boy rendered one beneath his feet and attempted to float out from the encasement, but the Priest anticipated it, rendering one of his own that pushed the boy back down, pinning him within the box like a lid slamming shut. The boy placed his hands frantically on each of the invisible walls, slammed against them, kicked them, and tried again to render his own, but none of them were as strong as the ones encasing him. His screams were silent. The box was airtight.

One of the Glasseyes stepped onto a square horizontal plane, bound with an upward force strong enough to support his weight. The Priest bound a direction and speed into it and it coasted gently across the canal with the Glasseye atop it. Even to Saya's eyes it looked as if he was levitating on his own, except that her proximity to the Slipstream meant she could feel the subtle vibrations of its shape and motion fifth-dimensionally.

"I know you are their Teacher," Sevastin Karda called out across the canal. "And I hope you can see everything."

The Glasseye removed a slender black needle from his leather satchel. The sharp end was corked, and resting inside a glass vial. He drew it out and removed the cork. The sharp tip dripped a black liquid.

Tinwood leaf resin.

She knew of it from her parents. It was how they kept magi docile and confused and disconnected from magick until it was convenient to burn them. It was usually administered in tea. But Khersas had taught her they sometimes use the powerful resin alone, for its effects were immediate.

The Priests nodded and the side of the cage the boy had his back to vanished. The Glasseye stepped in and gave him a single jab with the needle and then withdrew. The shield went back up, completing the cube once more.

The boy shook his head, dizzy, and held out both hands, steadying himself agains the invisible barriers. Then he slipped to his knees, lay down, and closed his eyes.

"We can do this to anyone, Teacher," Karda shouted. "You cannot stop this. Training them in the wild does not help them. You must give them to us. We train all human magi."

The Priests did not like to lie, she knew. It violated the very core tenet of their religion, insulting their sole deity. Yet it was a deceptive promise. A careful choice of words.

Because women magi are not human to you.

A clever way to cover up the fact that they burned the women right along with the grown men. They only saved the little boys to make into one of their own. Usually. They did not have to. Sometimes they executed them all.

Saya never once answered, nor gave away her hiding place.

The Priests dropped the walls of the box, and two of the soldiers lifted the boy and carried him away.

"We have eyes everywhere," Karda said across the water. "Sooner or later everyone is seen. Everyone is known in the end. Each person becomes truth. Even you."

He clearly did not know where she was. Nor did he seem intent on finding her. He did not order his soldiers or his Glasseyes to begin a search for her. He wanted her to go free knowing that he believed he could find her anywhere, and that he could undo all she had done.

"You will lead us to them all," he promised. "Nothing you do matters."

Those words cut her worse than any she had ever heard. It turned her heart black and her stomach into a hopelessly knotted cord. She slowly backed into a gap in the wall behind the cedars, and crossed a shady yard, squeezed between white stone houses, and fled.

The last thing she heard before she passed out of hearing range was Karda giving her one last sweet promise.

"I will find where you hide one day."

She stopped at the second safehouse. She traded robes. She lathered herself in ranum crystal soaps and scrubbed every inch of her body with a coarse brush until her skin was ready to bleed.

She cried a long time thinking of that poor little boy. She wondered if he would have gone on for years, perhaps a lifetime evading the Priests if she hadn't led them right to him. She found herself praying to Holy Juna to at least let them decide to keep him and train him to be a Priest, rather than execute him.

She would rather that sweet little boy become an implacable enemy bent on destroying her, rather than have him suffer any pain at their hands.

I will find where you hide one day.

She thought of how few days remained before they needed the money to bribe Jacobas to keep their little home grotto a secret.

If we don't think of something soon, we will not have a place left to hide.

She knew she and fifteen students suddenly tossed onto the streets would not last a fortnight. No shelter, no place to store food.

And it was impossible for magi to go extended periods without rendering something. Depriving a magi of their powers for more than a few days made them depressed, weeks and they would go mad, months and they would spiral into despair and end their own lives.

Khersas had said it happened to everyone. Saya believed him. She felt it herself when she tried for just two days. There was no way to win living out in the wide world. Sooner or later you had to use your magick, and every time was a roll of the bone dice whether or not you would be caught. And if you somehow restrained yourself from the addiction of using your own magick, you would do the work of the Priests for them.

We have to get the money. We have to think of a way.

And now things had just become worse. Any hope she had of foraging and trading herself just disappeared. Now that she knew they were watching the familiar areas for her, she could not simply walk the streets without subterfuge any longer, restricting where she could go and when.

An already impossible problem just became infinitely more difficult.

9

Thoughts Of Poison

SAYA MADE IT THROUGH the better part of the morning before she began to cry.

It was not merely because of the little boy she had failed, though that hurt her immensely. It was the accumulation of loss over her whole life rearing its head and gnawing upon her heart.

It began as it always did—with a beautiful memory. One that made her smile. That was the curse of loss. Not only would it take away the chance of any new memories, it would poison all the old ones by making you always remember there would be no more like them forever.

She thought of how Khersas had held her hand on the aqueduct lane, walking side by side, looking up at him, seeing one fallen star of an eye, one half of the dark curled jungle of his hair, and one half of that smile that could make her knees shake like sand caught in a breeze.

Thoughts of him could only last so long though.

Sooner or later every laugh and every sweet smile would bring her back to the truth that she would never see him again. Never scratch her fingernails down the scruff of his cheeks. Never slap him the way she did whenever he played pretend that he didn't love her. He never made it past the third slap before giving up the game and picking her up and spinning her around while she laughed with her eyes closed.

Eventually she always remembered that he was gone. And her heart would fall a thousand miles into the earth, cold, empty, like skin riding on pockets of air.

She would remember that she once had a mother and a father and a little brother and her heart had been full. And one by one they all went away. Her brother first. Then her father. Then her mother. Then Khersas.

When her thoughts began to spiral she would see each of their faces as happy as she could possibly remember them, swirling behind her eyelids like a dust devil, and she would rage against the unfairness of it. It wasn't right. It was unjust. Like the Priests. Like everything.

And then she would blink and be standing in the middle of the yard under a blanket of blue sky, embraced by safe red brick walls, surrounded by lovely trees and so many concerned little children.

Aafi came to her first, trotting over on those two little twigs he called legs, with a little orange bloom he had picked. In his other hand was, of course, a morning pastry. *Aafi, always the sweetest and the bravest. And the hungriest.*

After that it was a flood, each of the children vying to give her hugs and say they were sorry, even though they did not know what needed feeling sorry for.

Sotta made her smile by successfully binding his streams to render a bubble of silence about her. It was an area in space where the ability of waves to function was destroyed by rewriting one little piece of one of the laws of the universe, the one that allowed the energy of waves to be passed on. It was only the size of her upper torso, and only lasted for one minute, and was located in one place rather than tethered to her specifically, but it was an incredible achievement for someone so young. He said he had been practicing it all night to make her happy.

"Thank you, Sotta," she said, tapping his wide nose playfully with one finger. "You are the sweetest boy."

"Except for me," Aafi called out.

Saya rolled her eyes. "Truly, Sotta. You are doing so well." She motioned him in to whisper until he leaned his bald head in close. "The only other person I know who made a functional render of that size at your age was me." She winked at him.

His smile was as wide as a horizon. He walked away smirking at Aafi, prompting Aafi to hop after him, chirping questions regarding exactly what was the smirk about anyway?

Saya tried to smother her feelings, but her smile faded oh so quickly, replaced by a cold sickly stare to match the fear in her gut.

Tana brought her water, and Lili saved her a slice of the calpas fruit she had stolen from the market.

Raba gave her the three little copper coins he had been hiding in secret in a crack in the wall beside his bed all year, for no reason other than to have a secret, but he wanted to help however he could.

She shook his hand, ruffled his russet hair, and assured him that it would help make the difference.

Tashim gave her a list of all his meager belongings with an anticipated rate of exchange based on prevailing rates to sell them at the poormarkets. He had based everything on information Radir had provided him after his evening runs. Tashim even had a listing for his only blanket.

Saya's eyes squeezed out a tear before she could stop them. It was too much. Her beautiful little students were too much.

Mara was too shy to come forward on her own, but Adrani prodded her along. Mara did not have much, just hugs and tears. But it was enough. It was more than enough.

Serine followed with her own hug, and Faloush brought her his last cinnamon candy rope from when she brought him to walk the halls and smell the incense of the temple of Holy Juna. The temple-mistress handed out little bundles of them to each of the children on prayer days. They were Faloush's favorite treat.

Even the new boys, Beni and Timma, had made a little vignette for her out of twigs and leaves. It was a miniature of the layout of the compound, with the main house and the porch, Radir's shed, and the pile of debris out back. Each of the trees was represented by one of their leaves, and the little rocks in clay they painted red with the old bottle of dye from when she used to color textiles to sell, back before the Priests took over the highmarkets. Across the bottom they had written the word *home*. It was gorgeous and perfect and plucked the strings of her heart one by one. She embraced them both and thanked them for being a part of it.

Lastly came Qudra. He said he was sorry for always breaking the cups and costing them money and he really meant it and that saying so was his idea and that Radir certainly had not put him up to it.

She thanked them all and set them to their afternoon practice. When it came time for supper she could not eat.

Radir nodded to her and walked around the yard clapping his hands, drawing all eyes to him so Saya could sneak away by herself, without any of the others noticing.

She rendered an oval of lightbending refraction around herself and watched them from the stairs. She could have simply gone up to her room and looked out her window, but the act of rendering magick felt so good that she could not pass it up. Just touching the infinite light of the source was a salve for pain.

She needed her magick. She needed to be able to bind her streams or her heart would ache. After a full day of hiding who she was it felt like slipping into calm cool water to feel the bliss of touching the source and shaping magick to her heart's content.

She sat upon the halfway step and watched her beloved students, making sure that each of them was the happiest they could be and not just pretending so for her benefit.

They all took their favorite seats in the ring of mismatched old couches, faded red and dull yellow and worn green, each one frayed, each one full of holes. They spooned heaps of wheatmeal dashed with cinnamon from old polished stone bowls atop the table that was too high for the little ones and too low for the older students.

Sotta finished eating early, and strutted about, showing off his step-foot-hop dance as Adrani hammered out a rhythm with her knuckles and spoon, everyone clapping along as their splash of wheatmeal grew cold in their bowls. Tana and Lili giggled and clapped, hopping up and down on their cushioned couch seats, bouncing Serine up and down one seat over.

Tashim counted each of Sotta's steps and kicks and taps, keeping time with him in stomping feet. Qudra laughed and pranced after Sotta, trying and failing to do even half his footwork, exaggerating his moves until he was making a jest of himself. He received as many laughs as Sotta did cheers.

But it really was Sotta's hour. His rhythmic trotting and tapping and hopping enthralled Beni and Timma completely, chins in their hands, ready to follow him even if he led them on a jaunt into the sky.

Adrani stood and egged them on, her fist and spoon directing the music, her jet black braid writhing like a serpent over her shoulder, her smile as wide as a desert horizon.

Sotta was masterful, his wide calves agile as a goat's.

"Good moves that he does, when he moves that he does, that he moves," Raba said at double speed, speaking in circles and tying his tongue. He leaned over and smacked his palm on his head three times. "Too fast, too fast, too fast."

He was always harder on himself than anyone ever could be. Saya had been trying to work with him on speaking slower, but it was a long journey. He always wound himself up so tight and then let the words rip, stumbling, cheeks turning red as sunset.

Faloush wrapped him in a hug and rocked him back and forth three times until he calmed down and stopped hitting himself. Raba reached up and patted him on the head. Faloush smiled.

While the others were all distracted, Aafi systematically moved from place to place, his spoon trespassing in their bowls, twig arms sneaking in over shoulders and under hands, scooping all the extra bites he could into his mouth.

Mara noticed but she didn't say anything, biding her time no doubt.

When Qudra tired himself out, he worked his way around behind Lili and rendered magick on her orange, accelerating the effect of stress on a tiny portion of the underside of the peel, a straight line where the rind was now barely a tenth its strength.

Saya put her hand over her mouth to stifle a laugh.

Mara noticed this move as well, and this time she leapt up to try to warn her. But it was too late.

The orange opened up and juice and pulp dribbled and globbed out the bottom until Lili realized a good portion of her fruit treat was now in her lap. She flipped it over quick and set it on the low table, eyes scanning everywhere for Qudra.

Because she knew it was Qudra.

Because of course it was Qudra.

Qudra himself was already beating a hasty retreat out the front door, gently closing it to avoid drawing attention to himself.

Saya could not stop laughing, but by now the clapping and cheering were loud enough that it did not matter.

Night fell and Saya finally vanished up to her room before the last plate was clean. She listened to them singing songs, enjoying life, being happy. A place she could not go right now.

Her shutters were open already, but she did not mind. She wanted the open portal to the stars. She wished she could dive into the sky and swim its waters until all her pain had been washed away.

There was a dark ocean out there, a real one, somewhere beyond the sand. Khersas had told her of it, like the pond only larger, water so deep no one could touch the bottom, wider than all the steps she had ever taken put together. He had promised to take her to its beaches. The sands were different there, he had said, fine as silk underfoot, not at all like the rough desert sands her feet were used to. He had told her it was because the sea loved the land, smoothing it with its embrace, reaching out with rolling waves to kiss the shore.

How she longed to see it. But it was too far. That ocean and her future were one and the same. Always too distant to see. All she could do was look at the place she wanted to be and hope for someday.

Someday was not just a time. It was a place. Of peace and quiet where she could sit with her family again and trace the constellations of old across the azure vault.

We will go far away from here someday.

One of these tomorrows will lead us to a better life.

As long as the tomorrows keep coming, one of them will be that day.

And the good thing about tomorrows is that there always is one.

She spread her arms and tipped forward, collapsing into a sea of stolen blankets and thrown-away sheets. Hers now. Bounced barely at all on a mattress more quicksand now than cushion, but she loved the way it embraced her.

She put her face into the pillow and she screamed into it, crushing her mouth against it until her voice was no more than a squeak to her ears. To the pillow, she was raging and shouting and dying a thousand times. It knew all of her secrets, all of her pain, things no one would ever know.

It was all so deeply unfair—that Karda took away so much of the money, that he broke the cup, that he terrified her. That she was all alone. That she was the only one who could stand up for her students. That she had no one to share the burden with. That every day her back broke just a little bit more, until one day she would fold in half and never stand again.

She was tired. So tired.

She had her school and her students, and for that she was immensely proud. She had built something for herself and for them and she knew that should have been enough. But it wasn't. She wanted to run across a field of flowers just once, without having to always look over her shoulder.

Why did it have to be me? What was wrong with my family that you would take them away and not me?

The night air was cooling rapidly but she still felt hot, her hair coiled damp about her neck. She struggled to pull it all over her head. She slid out of her robes like pushing off into pondwaters from that splintery old post everyone used to climb out past the shallows.

She slid through her sheets like water, the kiss of moonlight on her skin. Her hands walked their way in its footsteps, across arms and shoulders, belly and hips, fingertips skipping across skin like stones across the pond. No matter the path they traveled, heat welled behind them, the ache of anticipation rising ahead of them.

She turned her face down into her pillows and groaned. Letting her volume rise. Again. Louder still. Her voice dry and full of breath, worn to scratches like the fringes of her only robes. She thought of Khersas' rough hands pinning her down, his weight upon her. She pretended her own exhales against the pillow were his breaths coming back to her, warming her lips, flushing her cheeks. She almost thought she could taste his kiss.

She pressed her hips down against the bedding, pinning her hand between. Her sheets became the dark ocean and she swam through its urgent twilit tides. Heat spread all through her as she tread euphoric swells, drowning in her own exhales, drifting across an endless sea, searching for oblivion. Every moan was full of aching need, each one a melancholy question with no answer. Her voice could not control her pitch and it spiraled out of control, chasing the sour pain in her heart higher and higher.

But the ocean she dreamed of revealed itself to be a wasteland of white sand, stale and cruel. She was chasing a mirage, vanishing every time she thought she had arrived, always just over the next dune. The sparkling water enticing her was a phantasm, leaving her only in endless desert, the surging wave she wanted never reaching shore.

She thought desperately of Khersas. She tried so hard to see his face, to keep him there with her in that moment, but it was futile. Nothing could undo this emptiness. Nothing could keep the sick rot of fear from filling the void. She cursed and screamed into the pillows, her angry fists pounding the bed.

It's not fair.

She could not even have this one small thing. One moment. One memory. Just one thing for her. One thing she was not doing for someone else. She could never have anything. She never would.

She beat the pillows and hammered the sheets. She sobbed recklessly, her eyes flooding. Until she remembered where she was and who might be able to hear, and so she stopped. Her frantic weeping could have upset the children, made them afraid. She did not even have the luxury to cry her own tears.

Her sobs ebbed until they became merely heavy breaths. She turned her head to the window and looked out at the silvery moon, Silistin shining back at her like the source.

She felt the sheets lift behind her and something warm slipped under the covers.

She smiled in spite of the raw pain behind her eyes.

It had to be Adrani. The girl had a knack for predicting when Saya needed comfort. She anticipated her arms wrapping her in a warm healing embrace, holding her still and quiet until she could close her eyes long enough to fall asleep.

But the hands she felt spreading out all across her body were all wrong, short stubby fingers rather than slender ones, coarse belly hair instead of smooth skin brushing her back.

Her eyes snapped open.

She flailed her arms, tossing the hands aside, and shaking loose of the body behind her. She rolled, pulling the sheets with her, cocooning herself amongst the linen as she rolled over.

No.

She saw Noqer on her bed in a way that she could not unsee, pose aggressive and sensual, eyes in shadow, spread out across her bedding.

Oh sweet Juna, no.

"Noqer." She said his name the way she did when she called upon him to answer a question in morning training. It was as much to gather the shards of her own thoughts as it was to remind him who she was and that he did not belong here at all.

He didn't say anything. He squirmed a few inches closer.

She shuddered, fighting back revulsion. Her stomach tried to empty its contents onto the sheets between them. It was horrifying.

"What?" he asked, squirming further.

"What are you *doing?*" She had to inch back until she was halfway to tipping out of bed to keep him from sliding into her arms.

How do I explain that this is inappropriate to someone who does not already know how obviously inappropriate this is? Without shattering them with embarrassment? How do I live each day under the same roof as what just happened here?

He reached out for her with one hand and she hopped away in disgust. The bed shook and the bedding rocked him back.

"No," she said.

He seemed shocked. "I came to give you my gift. To make you happy. To make you smile."

"Your gift? No. A flower is a gift. A hug is a gift. This is..."

"You always say how lonely you are," Noqer said. "You always say how much you miss Khersas in your bed. I heard you. You tell Radir and you tell Adrani, but I have heard you. I am a man now. I want to be the man in your bed. So you can stop being lonely."

"That is not how it works." She was so flustered and embarrassed and disgusted, and further embarrassed for *him* all at once.

Aya Jaytat, this cannot be happening. She could think of no other thing quite so awful and awkward as this.

She strained to keep her eyes looking off in shadow so that she would not have to see his body, his maximal arousal, thoroughly illumined by the silvery beams of the moon.

"You cannot be here like this. You cannot bring yourself into my bed. What is the matter with you?"

And yet she felt ashamed of her own carelessness in discussing such subjects where any of her students who were not ready to understand them might have heard.

"Is it because you think me a child?" he asked. "Like the others? Because I am a man now. I can show you."

She pressed her lips together to keep herself from gagging. "I know you are becoming a man, but this...this is not the way a man behaves." *At least not the way they should.*

"This is the way Khersas behaved. I saw him. I saw you. He slipped into your bed, just like this. I did it just the same way."

Saya felt her face flush. *He saw us. Aya Jaytat, Holy Juna, shine your light and save me from death by disgust and embarrassment.* "It is not the way it is done," she said, exasperated. "It is the person who is doing it."

"Am I not good enough for you?"

"I do not have those feelings for you," she said. "I cannot feel that way for you."

"But..." His voice stalled. His eyes became wide shadows. His face twitched in humiliation. "But you let Khersas."

"It does not matter," she said. "I do not think of you that way. Not at any age."

"But you used to sleep in the bed of Jacobas," he protested. "And you hate him. I do not understand."

She looked down in shame. "It is complicated."

"Do you not love me more than him? My body is strong. Jacobas is weak and ugly. Why not me?"

"It is that I do not have those feelings for you."

"But why?"

"Life is complicated. You will understand this one day. Understanding how complicated the world around us becomes is what growing up means. It is not the hair on your chin, or the feelings within, or who is in your bed. It is the *understanding* that makes you a man."

"But the way I feel," Noqer protested. "What I feel is real. What happens to me when I look at you. It is real."

"I cannot help the way you feel. But two must feel as one for what you want to be true."

His face twisted in anger. "Then there is no one for me."

Oh my poor sweet Noqer. She realized suddenly how there was a part of home that she had not thought out. She had created a perfect place, a sanctuary, where her students would never need to come in contact with any normals once they were off the streets. But that meant they would have no one but each other. She had forgotten that one day they all would grow up.

Noqer now. Soon it would be Adrani, begging to be allowed out to meet with boys by the pond, boys she might be foolish enough to trust with the secret of her magick. Mara was not far behind. But it did not matter. Soon they would all be here.

Noqer looked down at the floor, despondent. "I am humiliated," he said.

That makes two of us. "You are confused. You are becoming a man. You are changing and it is a confusing thing. I do not want you to feel humiliated, but you cannot do this ever again. Not to me. Not to any of the other girls who live within these walls. You invited yourself to my room without permission. You must never invite yourself into a woman's bed. You must wait for a woman to extend her invitation to you."

He recoiled from her, slithering off the bed and backing away toward the door. "I cannot believe this is happening."

"Go to bed, Noqer. We will not speak of this to anyone. None of the others have to know. We will talk about things in private tomorrow after the sun rises."

He did not say a word more. He backed away to the door and slipped out. She heard a rustle as he threw a robe over himself. She heard the creaks of his footsteps down the stairs and then he went out the door. She heard the patter of his feet crossing the yard to his room. And then silence.

She took three long breaths, held each one in, and exhaled slow.

She realized that eventually all of her students would grow up. Each of them would reach this same boundary of confusion. Each of them would rebel. Each of them would seek more outside these walls, or, as Noqer had done, be turned inward with calamitous effect.

What am I going to do? she asked herself over and over again. *What am I going to do about them? What am I going to do about Noqer?*

She could not even think of the first word she could say to him, especially when a part of her wanted nothing more than to pretend it had never happened at all, and just go on living the same as before. But she knew she could not. It was too dangerous to hide from it.

She put her head in her hands. *I should have talked to him sooner about how he was changing.* She realized she should have given Adrani's words more urgency. She had meant to, but she had been pulled in so many directions the past few weeks she had forgotten.

How am I to figure out how to talk to Noqer about these things when I cannot even figure out where our money will come from?

That fear pounded at the doors of her thoughts, forcing its way into her mind, shouting down everything else. She could concentrate on nothing else.

Where is the money going to come from?

10

Catching Stars

MIDNIGHT WAS BRIGHT WITH moonbeams, silver and blue splashing across the yard. She kept her upstairs window open, gazing out at the tops of the cedars, watching them try to climb into the sky and collect the stars.

Perhaps if you catch a star you could bring it down to me, she implored them. *So that I might use it as currency to keep this safe place as my home forever. So that I would not have to worry every day. So that I would not have to wear that exhausting happy face to keep the little ones from being frightened all the time.*

The night was cooled almost to comfortable by a night breeze, and she let it brush through her hair and tickle her skin like an invisible lover, comforting her in the night, dispelling her fear, shepherding her through the lonely darkness.

She heard a creak on her windowsill. It did not frighten her. She knew there was only one person alive who could scale the red bricks so quietly.

"Radir."

He hoisted himself up, swiveled his feet inside, and lowered himself into her wicker chair in the shadows. "I saw Noqer sneaking out of here. Was he stealing? Sneaking into rooms? Keeping the others awake?"

"I wish it was only one of those things," Saya said. "It would make things so much less complicated."

"Do you want me to dress him down?"

"No!" She barely kept herself from shouting. "No, it is something I will have to figure out how to deal with. Say nothing to him. Do not even mention it. Swear to me."

"I swear."

She smiled at the shadows of him. She loved him so deeply and completely. *Only he has truly seen the full measure of what awaits us outside these walls. Only he understands what I go through each day to keep this going, and the cost if I fail.*

There was a long silence.

"We do not have enough money, do we?"

Saya could not have hung her head any lower. "No."

"Do you have a plan?"

"No. He has never asked for this much before. And our luck finding coin has never been lower."

"We have always managed before. Something always comes through."

"I am stretched so thin, Radir. This worry is going to tear me apart."

"We have to look over our shoulders in this place. It comes with the territory. You leave to walk the city more than any of us."

"That's just it. I don't just have to look over my shoulder. I have to look over everyone's shoulder. Every time one of you leaves, I have to be sure no one has followed you back. I have to be sure you know your cleaning techniques so well that you never forget them. There is quite a leap between rarely and never. We cannot afford even one slip. Not even one. If one of us is happy or sad or angry or surprised or bored and we miss one little thing it is all over. Do you understand how exhausting that is?"

"You put a lot on your shoulders."

"I have no choice. We cannot lose this place, Radir. I have done so much work to make this a perfect place, to make it safe, to make it our own personal little hidden red and green grotto in the middle of a city full of harsh white danger. If I let a single thing go, the whole world comes crashing down on us. There is no part way. There is only all or nothing. I succeed because I have to. Whatever it takes. The alternative is losing it all."

"You need to rest sometimes. You cannot carry on this way."

"When do I have the time for rest? When food is needed on the table, and new shoes are needed on every pair of feet."

"You have to rest. You are going to collapse. Then you are no good to anyone."

She sighed. "When we get the money for this month I will rest, I promise."

He looked at her skeptically.

"I swear it, Radir. I'm just so..."

He looked at her a long time without answering. He turned to gaze out the window, at the pale stars above the red bricks and trees. "I meet a girl sometimes. Out on my runs. She sneaks me into a fenced yard off a back alley and she kisses me until I turn red. If no one is around we take our clothes off and play."

"I do not need that."

"I know you say you don't but I think you do. I think you do very badly. I think you miss being touched by someone who you love and who loves you back. In a way that is not just a part of a transaction."

Saya hushed him with a finger to her lips, lest Noqer should hear them talking and take the wrong idea from it all over again.

"It is always part of a transaction," she hissed, with more venom than she had meant to. "I loved Khersas so dearly, but even I know he would not have stayed with us as long as he did if I had not given him every bit of me."

"He cared about you."

"He cared about me enough to come see me once or twice. After that I made him come see me by giving him what he wanted."

"From what I heard the two of you get up to, he wasn't the only one who wanted it."

Saya was glad for the light of Silistin hiding her blush beneath a splash of silver. "I gave him what we both wanted. But I made him stay. He suffered through teaching the children with me, making runs with me, sharing responsibility with me. He did not do that out of love. He did that because I made this place worthwhile to him by always pleasing him enough that he did not stray, so that his thoughts did not need to wander to what woman he might see, or what adventure he might dream up. I kept him close. I made him ours. I had to. Yes, I wanted him. Yes, I loved him. But I know about men. I know about rogues. I know enough. I know they wander unless you can find some way to tie them down. And in Kasaban there is only one way to do that. I tied him down." She turned her face into her shoulder. "For as long as I could."

"We could leave," Radir suggested.

"Leave? Don't be stupid."

"Think about it. If we are not able to meet the price, then what? Jacobas turns us in. What then? Do we simply stay here? Perhaps we should plan for that. Perhaps we should just go now."

"Leave? Go? What are you talking about?"

"I am trying to think outside the box."

"It is not an option."

"Why not? You are the one who always tells me, you are only weak right now, not forever, leave now, come back stronger, fight again when you can win. If we can't win we have to leave."

"We would never survive. Travel across the desert costs even more than what Jacobas wants."

"We will find a way. Home is where we are. You protect the children here, you can protect them out there."

"No!" She nearly flattened him with her shout. She put her head in her hands, praying to Holy Juna that she had not woken any of the other children. She did not think she could summon the wherewithal to minister to their fears or their curiosities tonight with her mind as undone as it was.

Radir watched her carefully, unwilling to speak.

She settled amid her sheets and blankets, cross-legged, wearing them around her like a gown. "You do not understand. I cannot protect them by myself. I run my school, and I keep everything together, so you think of me as the strength of protection. But it is not me. It is the planning and arranging I have done. Purposeful. Meticulous. I created the systems that keep this place secret and safe, yes. But it is the *systems* of this place that protect us, not me."

"You are masterful at giving yourself all the credit while simultaneously giving yourself none of it." Radir chuckled.

She smiled at his laughter, but her lips flattened all too soon. "I told you about what happened to my brother."

"The Priests took him."

"Their Glasseyes found the afterglow of his magick with their little glass eyes and they followed us and they came for him."

"Yes. I remember."

"I told you that my father held me responsible."

"You did."

"But I never told you why."

"You do not have to."

"Yes I do. You need to understand. I told my parents that I could protect him on the streets. It was not so bad then. My brother and I had been drilled by our parents over and over about the invisible residue of our magick, our afterglow. How we could not see it, but the Glasseyes could. We both swore not to use any."

"What happened?"

"We spent the whole day out and it was wonderful. We played in the canal, we splashed in the fountains, and we bought sugar pastries from the confectioners' market. I had two because I was older. I gave my brother only one. He was so mad at me. He said it wasn't fair. But we only had the money for three and I was older and I told him to stop being such a baby."

"How old were you?"

"I was ten. My brother was six. I remember I turned my back on him. I felt so smug eating my extra treat, reveling in the fact that he was mad and could not do anything about it. But he could do something about it."

"He used magick," Radir surmised.

Saya nodded. "He made one of the pastries slide off the cart and into his hand. The confectioner saw him and called out to the magistrates. We ran as fast as we could. We thought we had got away. We had no idea back then that the Glasseyes had a way to track him from the afterglow he left back at the market."

"Spectral shift," Radir said. "You taught me about it."

"I did not know anything back then. I was surprised. I was terrified. I panicked. I used my own magick. I tried to protect my brother. That was what an older sister was supposed to do. It is what I promised my parents I would do."

She knew the tears would come. They always did when she thought about this part. Always. If she was dried-out bones buried in the desert, her skeleton would weep.

"We can stop," he said.

"You all think me so knowledgeable. I am your teacher. I can summon my patterns to unlock the door to the source faster than any of you. I can summon so many different streams from the source, such variety, you think me incredible."

Radir smiled. "You *are* incredible. Everything you just said is true."

"It may be," she said. "But it doesn't matter. Because no matter how many streams I can bind, how strong my renders can be, they have no mass. None. I can bend light, Radir. That is all. I can render shapes to change the dispersion of light. I can create fields where light does not behave the way it should. That is all."

"That alone is an incredible power."

"I used that power to protect my brother and myself. When they ambushed us, I rendered a bubble of invisibility around us. It was all I could do. It was all I could think of. I tethered it to him, and I pulled him along after me as I ran. The bubble moved where he did. And it was big enough to hide us both."

"I would have done the same thing," Radir said.

"But it is not perfect. I warp the light, but it is impossible to bend everything perfectly. They could see the distortion. All they had to do was reach inside and grab him. And they did. My magick could not even offer as much resistance as a square of linen. My protection was worthless. I am the one who failed. I thought I was so strong. But my strength was an illusion."

"You cannot blame yourself."

"The way my father did? I do not remember him ever smiling at me again after that."

"You did the best you could. Of that, I am sure."

"I did. But you see, Radir, that is just it. My best could do nothing against them. My best is what lost my brother." She dragged her hand through a beam of moonlight. "I cannot protect them by myself. I am not strong enough. I cannot shield people, I can only hide people. That is what I do. The last time I tried to protect someone, I lost that person forever. I cannot do that again."

"Saya..."

"I built this place instead. I paid to have the entrance hidden. I learned every way I could to fool the Glasseyes. I used my mind and my body to outwit them. I found a system that could stop them before they ever saw me. That is what this place is. That is why I cannot simply take fifteen children and rent a room at the old hostel. Because there would be nothing there to protect them. Nothing but me. And I alone am not enough."

"You will find a way. Like you said. You will think of something. You needed a place. You needed a system. You needed a set of rules. You needed a certain set of circumstances to exist. You made it happen, Saya. You worked hard and you solved that problem. You can do it again. You can solve this problem as well."

"Without a safe place, I can offer them nothing. I tried to defend my family once. I failed. Now I have no family."

"Wrong. Now *we* are your family. You protect us. Some day you will defend your family. Some day you will not fail."

"I don't know, Radir. I just don't know."

"You must leave all the other problems behind. None of the rest will matter if we cannot solve this one. We do not have enough money to pay off the man who keeps the warren-bosses from sniffing around here. What can we do about it?"

She was silent a long time, thinking about what Noqer said to her. "Offer him something else." *Offer him me.*

"Would he take such an offer?"

She shook her head. "I could make him bend his rules, but not break them."

"Then that brings us to the option of killing him, and worrying about the fallout of that when the time comes."

"The fallout. It would be dangerous. Not only would the warren-boss hand over this territory to someone else who might wonder why this place has four walls and no doors. But that is if we even make it that far. I have to believe a warren-boss would send some of his crew to investigate a missing man. What happens when they find us? Kill them as well? The cold truth is that Jacobas does not merely look the other way and pretend not to see us, he keeps others from looking for us at all. With him gone that would end. Who knows if the next one will be as weak-minded as him. Like it or not, and I definitely do not like it, Jacobas is a part of this system I have built to keep us safe. Without him, it all begins to unravel."

"That leaves but one other way."

"What way?"

"We find the money somehow."

Saya stifled a laugh. "Find that much? In just three days? How?"

"There has to be a way."

Saya released a full-throated laugh into the night air. She laughed at the futility of it all. *After all this work, after all this preparation, to be defeated by one small man.* It was more than she could bear. "We would have thought of one by now."

Radir made a face at her. "We were thinking inside the box. We were thinking of doing more of what we already do. What about something else we have never done before? What about something wholly new?"

"I am up for ideas," she said.

"Wager what we have at the dice dens?"

"None of us are good at gambling. If we lose we would be worse off than we already are. And the kind of places that play to those stakes are the kind frequented by those who would mug us and steal our money before we had a chance to bet it."

Radir shrugged.

"Terak says we should steal from the other pickpockets." She laughed. "Since they would not be able to call on the law. *Why not steal from the thieves?* he asked me." She laughed a little.

Radir laughed, too. "Terak is wise." He looked away. "Perhaps we could hit the line at the Moneychanger. All the thieves go there to change denominations."

She chuckled at the absurdity of the thought. Anyone who tried to rob the poorchanger would be torn to pieces by the mob waiting in line. That place was like a god, who convinced the masses to fight and kill for it, to ensure it would always be there to turn their money so the people could pay their debts. "The Moneychanger is the greatest thief of all."

He glanced at the walls, and then the roof over their heads. "Having seen the miracle you have created with this place, I no longer believe anything is impossible."

"Catching stars, my father used to call it." Saya reached toward the window, trying to scoop handful of them out of the night sky. "Whenever my brother and I would keep trying at something futile, rather than simply accept the way things were and move on. The answer we are reaching for is but a dream. We are catching stars, my wonderful friend."

He sighed solemnly, hands on his knees. "There has to be something."

"You can say it until it snows in Kasaban," she said. "Wishing won't turn sand into water."

"I refuse to believe our life here is over," he said.

She laughed so she wouldn't cry. "It is hopeless. Nothing would do it save for if I went to break our silvers at the Moneychanger and the box man mistakenly gave us a pile of golds instead of coppers."

Even Radir laughed at the chances of that. It was like trying to make the sun go backwards.

"We will have to plan for what happens when Jacobas tells on us then," Saya said. "We will have to be prepared."

"I will begin scouting our cleaning stations," Radir said. "We can use one of them as a temporary place to hide until we can find someplace new."

The very idea of planning to leave home brought a wave of tears to her eyes. This was the place she had built. This was the place her work had made. She loved every inch of this place—every branch of every cedar, every red brick, every creaky old stair, the torn screen of the door, the little shed, every orange from the orange tree.

Every single patch of grass was a place where she had a cherished memory of one of her students doing something exceptional to make her proud. How could she turn her back on a place of such luscious memories?

"Radir?"

"Yes?"

"I don't want to leave."

"I know."

"It will be hard on the children."

"They will get through it. We will get through it."

"Thank you, Radir. For always being here for me. I do not know what I would do without you."

He looked away out her window, smiled in the moonlight. "I just wish there was a way to make the Moneychanger give us that pile of gold coins."

She smiled, too.

He began to laugh.

So did she.

He laughed harder.

So did she.

He settled into a low chuckle.

She stopped laughing.

He continued to chuckle.

She was not laughing at all now. She was silent.

Radir noticed. "What is it?"

Why not steal from the thieves?

She stared through him, out the window, up into the sea of stars. "I think I know a way we can get the money."

11

To Steal From The Thieves

NO ONE HAD EVER robbed the Moneychanger before.

Saya intended to be the first.

She had to wait for a day that was both windy and bright for even the first step in the plan to be possible. Sunlight was not a problem. Rarely were there more than a few clumps of billowing cloud in a Kasaban sky. But the wind was another matter. Sometimes it howled and sometimes it was still.

Luckily, on the morning of the final day before Jacobas required his payment the winds blew hardy and continually. She needed the sun and the wind to conspire to mask the afterglow well enough that it would not be noticed.

Saya whispered a prayer for good fortune to Holy Juna as she led her students through the scorched city streets. Sunlight scraped her skin. She kept a linen hood up over the back of her head as a shield against it, her obsidian hair tucked into a lazy braid beneath. The air smelled of ripe mud and old clay, powdered white with a sheen of desert dust.

Heat surged against her, drowning her in feverish exhaustion, every seventh step another drop of sweat skimming down her body to become lost in the cloth bunched around her rope belt. Every exhale stole her water, a looming threat of dehydration she had no way to stop. They had to make it to shade before too long.

Her students were handling the heat much better than she was. They were thrilled to be out of the walled-in safety of the school. Once they reached the highmarkets, they each shed their sackcloth covers to reveal the finest clothes that hands could steal.

First came Mara in a pale white robe with short sleeves, her hair cut short like a brown bowl atop her head in the fashion of the exalted virgins of the Sorai Resa. None were permitted to glance at one of them, their bodies reserved for one of the ruling class to marry. Saya hoped that would keep eyes away from her long enough.

A sullen Noqer followed her in one of Radir's best and brightest shirts, his sour embarrassment temporarily subdued by Saya's assurances of how important his magick would be for this to work. She had agreed to talk with him after it was done, really talk to him, about how he was changing on the outside, and what he was going through on the inside. She had promised him they would work out some way for him to spread his wings. He seemed mollified. Saya was relieved.

Aafi and Qudra followed wearing the matching brown breeches and warm ivory wool shirts Saya had sewn for them from scrap cloth and thrown out spools from the textile creationary.

Tashim brought up the rear with Sotta and Faloush, each wearing the new terra-cotta colored jerkins they had stolen from Faurage tailors the day before. They were finer clothes than any Saya had ever worn, all silky soft linen. It had been a risk to take them, but the three boys needed to appear harmlessly well-to-do in order to escape the notice of the elites, not be garbed in the scraps and rags of a thieving sewer rat.

They needed to pass as wealthy, enough to fool a glance or a squint. They needed to be able to walk in the middle of the street, to look like they were not searching every crowd for a pocket to pick.

All the nicest streets of Kasaban were filled with suspicious wards or private guards, the Ministry acolytes or city governor's street soldiers, whose eyes would be like glue upon anyone radiating poverty. She marveled at how good it would feel to not have brooms swiping at her ankles, those piles of white sand and dust heaped over her sandals.

When they spilled onto a main thoroughfare, here students were all suddenly quiet, doing their best to imitate the austere poise of the children of the wealthy. Even wisecracking Aafi was silent as a ghost.

It was difficult for children who were as used to hiding and sneaking as they were. Here there were no places to hide. Every edifice was high solid white stone, with grey beams and pale red roofing. What few plants there were tended to be skinny palms and half-dead scrub. There would be no hiding here after it was done. They would need to run or die.

Her students spread throughout the crowd, filtering among the opulent merchants in rainbows of satin and city officials in pure white silks studded with silver badges.

Saya followed just behind them, keeping them all in view. Adrani, Mara, Aafi, Qudra, Tashim, Sotta, and Faloush. These were the students she knew could focus best under pressure, and each brought a different talent to bear. She had made certain they all ate hearty breakfasts, eggs and cheese, potatoes and beans, she even let them use one of the onions. It was important that they all be full and well-rested to have as much energy as possible to render magick before undertaking such a desperate plan as this. She could not have them collapsing halfway through.

She had spent every day planning and forcing her students to practice what they were to do. They needed to be calm, relaxed, focused. They had to be in perfect sync for this to work.

She forced Radir to remain behind. *If anything happens to me the children will need someone older to protect them and guide them and to make sure they practice.*

Raba and Tana, Serine and Lili, Beni and Timma, all too small, too weak, or too poor with concentration. Or all three. They would not survive without some older children to watch over them.

In case we don't make it.

In case I fail.

Please, Holy Juna, do not let me fail.

She knew it was a gamble. But time had run out. They had only until nightfall before Jacobas expected his payment. It was all or nothing.

She walked herself through what she was going to say, what she was going to do, over and over, until she knew it so well, she could do it by accident.

Three blocks to go.

I am not ready.

She pinched her arm.

I am ready.

She turned down a final alley leading to the avenue of the Moneychanger. She chose the one behind the old blind butcher's home, yearning to see the flowers in the little pot in his back garden, where her father had once plucked one each for her and her mother back before her brother had been born.

She did not see any flowers.

The garden was gone.

There were two young men standing in front of her instead.

She stopped so suddenly she nearly snapped her ankles. Her breakfast wanted to throw itself out her mouth. She felt her heart in her ears. Thumping. Deafening.

They were as tall as men, but in truth they were no older than she. Each held a hammer and chisel.

Carving graffiti.

Their faces were both long and snarled like gruff desert dogs, and their clothes smelled as bad as their intentions. They wore matching red vests. The rest of their clothes in tatters, but not the vests. They were new. Like uniforms.

These are the foot soldiers of a warren-boss.

She realized she was still standing there, frozen. She wished she should have kept walking past them. *Why couldn't I just keep walking past them?*

The first one took a step toward her. "See what fortune brings us?" he said. A liar's smile spawned across lips as wet as fresh dung.

She tried to walk past him, but he sidestepped, blocked her path, staring her down. He extended his arm, placing his palm on the wall of the tenement he had only just been defacing.

His eyes were full of want, screaming silently about what they deserved. He looked her up and down, smiling cruelly, mischievously. The other stood behind him, united in ill intent.

She summoned her most severe stare to match his. Oh, how she wanted to slip into the source. She felt her streams calling to her. *Let us make you invisible. Let us help you escape. Let us help you win.*

But she could not. Not when she was this close.

He licked his lips. His eyes tried to crawl around under her robes.

"Do you intend to keep me all to yourself?" she asked. "Or will you allow your friend a turn?" She pointed to his friend behind him. She could see desire already in his trousers, and a deep want in his eyes. "See? He may want to share."

As soon as the first one turned to look back at his friend, Saya ducked low under his outstretched arm and was away past him. He spun all the way around and reached after her, but too late. His companion was so stunned he merely stood still.

"Come, children," Saya said.

Before the two young men could react, her students sped past them, bumping into them as they ran. The two boys shouted, but Saya flowed into the wide avenue, where wealthy morning foot traffic was plentiful and warren rats dared not tread. The two boys never came after them that she could tell.

Her students immediately dispersed into the crowd, walking in the middle of the street, feigning wealth and privilege.

Saya was preoccupied watching every bobbing head in the crowd. A part of her was expecting someone to turn and corner one of the children, to accuse them of impersonation.

Every wealthy merchant lady stepping around a corner in a white robe was Sevastin Karda, at least until Saya could prove it was a human face and not a gold mask.

It will all be over soon, she swore to herself. *Only a few minutes and we shall be on our way home.*

She could already see the tiled roof with its two tall wind towers, catching the warm breeze and funneling it down into a basement of cold water pools before drafting back up into the hallways of the Moneychanger to moderate the temperature. They were easily recognizable rising above the houses even from three streets away.

She had sent Radir to scout the location and study the schedules. She knew when the deliveries were made. She knew when the lines were long, and when they were closed for meals. She had required as much information as possible to plan this. It had to work. There would be no second chance.

Adrani had already stocked three of the stops on the path home with changes of clothes, wash basins full of water, buckets of cleaning crystal soaps and shimmering sand, light sticks and rosewood to smoke their hair and skin. The clothes she and the children wore now would be discarded or burned. After what they intended to do today, every possible caution would be necessary to avoid being found by the Priests and their Glassdogs.

Saya stopped at the mouth of an empty alley across the street from the front wall of the Moneychanger, studying the high-walled patio, black iron gate in the center, offering the only way into the compound. The line for the poorchanger's table out in the street wrapped around the corner, and the streets were packed. Scaling the wall would be impossible without everyone noticing immediately.

Both gate and wall were taller than Saya, but not quite as tall as the heavy brute that stood guard outside. He was broad of shoulder and dumb of expression, and looked out of empty glazed eyes, watching the crowd the way an old lighthouse keeper watches the sea.

Here she waited with Adrani, timing the traffic on the wide avenue, each of her students in her periphery.

Aafi, Qudra, and Noqer walked casually up and down the street, waiting for the right moment. Each had a pouch tied to their belts with what little crystal soaps they had at home.

Mara paused between two ferns decorating a nameless statue in the wall one building further on, pretending to recite a religious mantra so she would be left alone.

Saya motioned for Sotta, Faloush, and Tashim to stand beneath the ancient sign dangling from old chains above a water purifier's front door, wearing their fine, freshly-pilfered raiment, trying their best to impersonate the spoiled children of some wealthy craftsmen while they waited for her signal.

Saya swayed with the movements of the crowd, listening to the twittering glissades of the hectic sparrows in the luxurious shade trees bestride the Moneychanger's patio.

When she saw the deliveryman at the end of the street, she whistled to Mara to move in close to the brute guard. The girl did her best to look innocent.

When the deliveryman moved past the water purifier, she signaled to her three boys with a wave, and they started to follow him, blending in and out of the crowd with all the skill they had honed cutting purses.

Saya held her breath for what seemed minutes, the sparrow songs swelling in her ears. Aafi, Qudra, and Noqer were looping around to make another circuit of the street. They noticed Mara and worked their way obliquely through the crowd to meet her at the gate.

The deliveryman was so close now, easily recognized in a blue tunic and red cape. He carried a heavy bag over one shoulder. Within it sat a cumbersome quantity of notes and papers and orders, foodstuffs and purses for the wealth within.

The deliveryman reached the gate. The brute eyed him mutely and turned a key in its lock. The gate swung inward, allowing the deliveryman to step through.

The timing had to be just right. Saya was shaking, fingernails spearing calloused palms. Every breath felt solid, her exhales plummeting to the ground like vomited bulbs of stone.

The brute released the gate and it began to drift closed. With it went their one chance.

Saya could not tell whether she was breathing. She could have retched her heart out onto the ground at her feet and not noticed it at that moment.

She prayed to Holy Juna to grant her students luck and good timing.

Please shine your light upon us, Holy Juna, today of all days.

Faloush had the best aim. He was the natural choice to throw the dirt clod. He had painstakingly molded it from mud and soil down by the edge of the pond, and held it in his pocket all morning, waiting for this very moment.

It struck the brute in the side of the head.

He turned. Saw Faloush. A snarl spread across his face.

Saya began crossing the street, while the other children— Noqer, Aafi, Qudra, and Sotta—converged on the gate. Only Adrani remained behind, to act as lookout when they came back out after the job was done.

Tashim plucked the stopper from a bottle of fish oil Terak had sold them at half-price. He handed it to Faloush.

He threw the open bottle.

The brute raised his arm and blocked the bottle, but that only served to shatter it on his iron bracelets. The glass turned to shards, spilling the foul fish oil all across his chest and face.

The brute growled and reached after Faloush.

Faloush turned tail and ran. The brute was full of rage. He swept past Tashim and hurtled down the street after Faloush.

The deliveryman turned back to see what was amiss.

Mara slipped behind him.

Now, Mara!

Mara stood stone still, the patience of a mountain, focused as a desert blade. She was Saya's best concentrator. She bound streams. The stream of *position* Mara pulled into the bind had to be just perfect to place the render of her brightest magnitude of light into reality right where his eyes were focused. Saya believed in her. If anyone could do it, Mara could.

It all took less than a second.

Suddenly a bright flash of light sparked into reality directly before the deliveryman's eyes. He cursed, his hands feeling around blindly.

The flash lasted for less time than it had taken to render it. So quickly did it fade, that no one else on the street even noticed it. But it was long enough to blot out the deliveryman's vision for a few moments, forcing him to set the supply bag down and rub at his eyes. Long enough for Saya to step right up to him. Long enough for her to pantomime speaking and gesturing with her hands without him seeing her there. Long enough for Mara and Noqer and Sotta to rush through the closing gate. Long enough for Aafi, Qudra, and Tashim to follow.

To the people in the streets it looked like the deliveryman was having a friendly conversation with her, and very obviously permitting her children inside. The bright sunlight hid any visible afterglow from Mara's magick, and the wind helped disperse what unseen portion remained.

Saya glanced over her shoulder. The brute was stalking back down the street, grumbling defeat, his size and strength no match for Faloush's nimble feet. He was still shaking his fists and rubbing at his eyes.

At last Saya herself stepped through the gate as it swung the final few spans, the latch tapping but not clicking shut. Once inside they all ducked into shadowed corners of the well-manicured gardens flanking the stone path between the gate and the Moneychanger's front door, blending into vines, ferns, and cedar branches.

Saya huddled beside Mara under the branches, giving an encouraging shake to her shoulders. *I am so proud of you.*

The deliveryman finally located the gate with his meandering hands. He yanked it shut behind him with a rusty clang. He stood still, blinking for his sight to return, rubbing his eyes with his palms.

The brute returned to the gate, and the deliveryman exchanged a confused glance with him through the bars. The brute shrugged angrily, cleared his throat, and passed wind, then returned to his post outside, allowing the patio to settle back into its usual silence.

The deliveryman looked all around, thoroughly befuddled. He sighed, picked up his supply bag, and walked down a short path beneath an overhang to the front door. He flipped a key from one of his pockets, turned the lock, depressed the latch, and disappeared inside. The door clicked gently shut behind him.

Stealth was their friend. There would be no Glasseyes within the compound of the Moneychanger. If they could keep their renders small, low magnitude, and unobtrusive, the afterglow would be less, unlikely to sensitize what it touched, and fade sooner. If they could clean whatever they touched with their hands, no one would ever know.

Saya steadied herself. There was not much time between the delivery and the arrival of the afternoon customers. They had to go now. Cautiously, they crept out of the bushes and went to the door. Saya tested the latch just in case. Locked.

Tashim went to work immediately, rendering a series of very tiny spheres before the keyhole. His skill level did not allow him to put great mass into them, but he was more precise with his position and direction streams he could bind into his renders than anyone she had ever known.

Hopefully their velocity would translate into enough force to shatter the lock mechanism, allowing him to slide the bolt free. If it didn't work, they would have to hope that Qudra could apply enough stress to the metal that they could force it by hand, but that would take longer and be far more conspicuous.

As it was, Saya kept a watchful eye out toward the gate from under the overhanging roof of the patio, making certain she saw the top of the brute's head poking up above the top of the wall. If he heard them at all, the plan went to ruin. Sotta could have layered renders to absorb their small sounds, but she could not afford to have him use up all his strength this early on.

With a sequence of tiny pings, Tashim's little spheres snapped apart the internal components of the lock. He tested the latch as he went until it finally ceased to offer resistance, and the bolt slid out.

Saya panicked at each ping. The tiny sounds were each a thunderclap in her ears. She gave herself a headache straining her eyes to glance at the brute without turning away from the door. But he did not hear.

She pressed her ear against the door, cool and smooth. She heard nothing. No one was coming. She inched the door open. Peeked inside. A blast of cool air washed over her, so delightful that she involuntarily closed her eyes and leaned her head back, biting her lip. *Sweet Juna, it feels so good.*

She forced her focus to return. *No distraction. You knew it would be like this. Stop it. Hold yourself together.*

Dark within. No windows at all, only oil lamps. Even those were few and small. The darkness would be both a blessing and a curse, but at least the hallway was open and unguarded. She held the door until all her students were within, then made one final check of the gate to be sure the brute was unmoved before pulling it closed.

They followed a brief hallway with closed doors to either side, terminating at an intersection with another corridor running perpendicular to it. But their hallway ended there. Directly ahead was a wall with a single door.

Saya checked around the corner on either side. Both were empty. So many of the staff must have been away at their meals. It was better than she could have hoped. The gate and the lone brute and the locked door were nothing but a facade. Beyond it the security was abysmal, bordering on nonexistent. No guards, no patrols, no barriers. As if the whole of their security was rooted in hoping no one would try to do this simply because no one ever had.

She heard a sudden rustling behind her. She went still. Each of her students did the same. The deliveryman stepped out of one of the side doors they had already passed. He carried a crumpled and deflated leather bag, having disgorged its contents within. He pulled the door closed and went for the front door to leave.

Saya tasted acid in her mouth. Her sweat turned to ice.

He withdrew his key and tried it in the lock. It slid through fine, but he made a confused face. He slid the key back out and in and out again, and finally slid it in and turned it. It did not click, but the door opened. He let out a breath and shook his head. He slipped out the door and did the same game of pretending to lock the door again from the outside.

He clearly noticed the lock was not working, but luckily he was lazy and frustrated enough to leave it to be someone else's problem. He never once looked down the hallway behind him to notice Saya and her six students.

Saya stifled a laugh. Her fear made her giddy.

Saya returned her attention to what lay ahead. The door to the office of the Moneychanger was directly ahead in the wall at the cross of the T. It wasn't even locked. She opened the door easily.

The room beyond was lined with shelves full of musty folios and record books, with a desk at the center, a vial of ink and a quill atop it. Beyond the desk was another door. Saya remembered what was inside. She had seen that door open before, many years ago, peeking through the legs of her parents when she was but a child, seeing the bars and the coins.

She crossed the room. Her children followed her around the desk, except for Aafi, who decided that he had to crawl under the desk for no reason but his own. This door, too, opened without resistance, and Saya was at last within sight of that which would save their home.

She brought all of the children inside and closed the door, setting Sotta immediately to render a layer of invisible baffles, rewriting the laws of the universe so that sound waves would not pass through the areas he decided.

Saya hoped they would prevent soundwaves from moving the air beyond that point, preventing any small noises they could possibly make from escaping out the door and out into the hall. Saya hoped it would be enough to absorb the noise of their hurried robbery. It would do nothing to prevent vibration through the walls themselves, though, so they still as yet required the utmost caution.

She then set her sights on the final barrier—the cage. It was a crisscrossed lattice of iron bars stretching from wall to wall and floor to ceiling. There was no clearance around it, under it, or over it. The open squares of space were too small to fit a cat through, let alone one of the children.

Beyond the bars sat a table, three plump bags of coins beneath it. They were all full and unopened, but far too large to fit through the bars. She ignored them anyway. She had not come here for sacks of copper.

Her eyes were instead drawn to something else. Upon the table stood an ostentatious money counter on four carved wooden legs, each one a rampant griffon, with half-open cylindrical spaces to stack coins of various denominations. They were all at least half-full, most of the stacks of good Naphesan silver, and at least one of the finest Hidiom gold currency from the Corien Empire, the same empire that sent its Priests to turn Kasaban into their next province.

Now their imperial money would pay to liberate her small family. Just two of those coins would buy off Jacobas for half a year. They would never want for anything ever again.

Saya turned to Qudra. "Your turn. You can do it."

Qudra concentrated, his brow furrowed, his hands balled tightly into fists at his side. He shook as he struggled against fear to unlock the Slipstream. He gritted his teeth to dip into the source. He closed his eyes as he felt around for the streams that were natural to him, selecting ones he desired, declining others. He bound the preferred streams together until they were one singular effect that he could then render into reality, changing one small constant within one specific equation of the mathematics that ruled the universe.

He drove up the natural stress acting upon the legs of the money counter until it was at incredible levels. The four carved griffons of its legs quivered as if they had just aged a hundred years.

Still it was not enough.

Saya bit her lip. "Noqer, go," she said.

Noqer bound his streams into a render. He altered the mass of the counter itself until it weighed as much as twenty blocks of lead.

The legs now temporarily aged a hundred years *and* held up something weighing a hundred times as much. The combined efforts finally compromised the integrity of the front legs of the money-counter, snapping them like twigs. The entire counter tipped forward, slamming down on the table like a cymbal splash. The cylinders holding each stack of coins held fast, only permitting three silvers to shake loose and roll free. They spun across the table and dropped to the floor. They rolled all the way to the bars of the cage. Mara reached her hand through and snatched them up.

Saya waved Aafi forward. "Can you make them slide out of the stacks?" she asked. "If you decrease the friction acting on them, they will slide out, fall off the table, and roll to us."

Aafi nodded. "I can do that." He stared at the coins as if starving for them.

"Tashim," Saya said. "Can you render spheres into the side of it to rattle the coins loose?" It was rhetorical. She knew he could. They had been practicing that very thing not a month ago. "Be careful. Remember, only a tiny bit of speed. We do not want them to become missiles, nor for the money counter to move or spin."

He chewed his lip, no doubt remembering when he had accidentally done that very thing with the dishes.

Saya watched her students combine their renders with a coordination that made her so proud to behold. The stacks received a gentle jolt, then another, and another, and with the natural friction of the cylinders reduced to zero, one by one the coins slid loose and dropped onto the table. They rained down on the floor, rolling every which way.

Saya and Mara both began snatching up any and all coins that came within reaching distance through the bars. They heaped them into little metal piles, and scraped them by the handful into empty stockings until they had a half-dozen of them tied off and bulging.

When all of the coins had finally fallen, Saya rose to her feet and stepped through Sotta's noise-absorbing renders. They did not affect her at all, only waves of air. To her and the children they might as well not have been there at all.

She smiled at Sotta. His face was bright red, sweat streaming down his cheeks. His breaths were taken in wheezing gasps. Saya wiped his forehead with the sleeve of her robe, and patted him on the head, smiling. "You did so well, Sotta."

He smiled back exhaustedly.

She set them to cleaning the surfaces they could reach, wiping them with rags wet with crystal soaps and sand, leaving as little trace as possible. She knew they would not open the vault until the next day. It needed to appear as an accident combined with a bookkeeping error. With luck, and Holy Juna's blessing, they would not even know it was a crime needing to be reported.

With all of her students nearing exhaustion, it was finally time for Saya to render. She pulled the door softly open, verified the room beyond was still empty, and the other door still closed. She crossed the room, skirting the desk. Her hip clipped one corner of the desk and it moved an inch across the floor, its feet squealing. Saya felt her heart stop, then start again. But no one heard. Her sigh of relief was heavy enough to crater the earth.

She put one hand to the door, then bound her streams, rendering a cocoon of light-bending in an oval around herself, slender enough to pass through the doorway without touching the sides. It curved and refracted light around her, showing anyone from any direction a warbled version of what was on the other side of the bubble, making her into a walking blotch of invisibility, like a rippling translucent prism.

She pulled the door wide. Looked both ways. Straight ahead at the end of the hall stood the door to freedom. To the left there was nothing. To the right stood a man, fiddling with one of the oil lamps. He glanced her way when he heard the door creak, but he did not look too closely and went back to his fiddling.

Saya stepped invisibly into the hallway. Once in the hallway, she swapped out the stream controlling the circumference of her bubble, binding in its place one of greater size. He bubble expanded until it was as wide as the hallway, without touching the walls.

One by one, her students filed out of the room into the protective invisibility of the bubble, hugging themselves to her to keep within its bounds.

She guided her students past the man and down the hall. She maintained the bubble until they reached the front door, safely out of sight of the man fixing the lamp. There she released her lightbending bubble by swapping a stream of *duration* of zero into the bind.

She pushed open the front door, ushering the children out onto the patio and back to the gate. The head of the brute was still there, poking above the wall.

Her plan of escape from here was eloquent in its simplicity. Its main ingredient would be the gullibility of the brute. She rendered a flat rectangular reflective wall perfectly perpendicular to the stone wall itself. She placed it between the brute and the gate just as she pulled the gate open behind him, with a duration of five seconds.

The gate whined and squealed as it opened, but when the brute turned to look for the source of the sound, he only saw his own face reflected back at him.

Saya and her students walked calmly past him, hidden behind the mirror, joining the morning traffic. The brute reached out one finger at his own reflected face, but the duration of the render expired and the reflection blinked out of existence.

The brute scratched his head. The sun drowned out the shimmer, and the wind degraded and dispersed the invisible glow. No cry of alarm rang out. No shouts or curses. It had worked perfectly, better even than Saya had imagined it would.

The streets seemed pleasantly normal. She maneuvered obliquely through the crowd until she was across the street one block further up. She rounded a second corner into a narrow connecting passage between the alleys.

There Adrani and Faloush waited for her. Faloush jumped up and down excitedly as soon as he saw her, little sandals clapping against the cobbles.

"You're back! You're back!" He said. "Did you get it? Did you get it?"

Saya held her finger to her lips and shushed. "Not now, Faloush. We must go now."

Faloush frowned, disappointed. "But did you get it?"

Saya rolled her eyes at him, but she smiled. "Yes."

Faloush clapped and smiled back. Saya reached out to pat him on the head.

Then the fist hit her.

Her head snapped to the side and her vision went black. She dropped to one knee, one hand reaching out to the nearest wall. Her fingernails chipped as they scraped against the bricks. Her tongue turned to rubber. Her knees melted like butter in the sun. Rough hands shoved her to the ground.

When her vision returned, sparks floated in her eyes. She saw Mara holding her hand up to her mouth, terrified. She saw Aafi and Qudra, jaws open wide enough to swallow a sand dune.

Saya did not understand. The plan had worked. They had gotten away. No one even knew they had been there. How had it gone wrong?

She turned to look up and saw two older boys. Tall and lean. Hungry. A third boy held both of Adrani's wrists pinned above her head with one hand, choking Sotta against the wall with the other. His face was a mask of mischievous fury. Sotta struggled, face purple, gasping for breath. He shook Sotta a few more times, then dropped him.

She recognized the red vests. The same vandals they had ducked past on the way here. When the lead boy noticed Saya looking at him, he grinned and stomped over to her. Kicked at her sharply in the hip. Saya winced and cupped a hand at her leg.

"What did you get?" he asked her, mimicking Faloush.

No. This can't be happening. Not now. Not when we are so close. Her eyes stung. Her hands shook. She could not bring her focus to bear no matter how hard she tried. Every time she tried to bind her streams together the pain in her temples forced it back down.

The boy kicked her again.

Mara reached out protectively, but one of the other boys slapped her hard on the cheek, and she fell on her side.

Qudra ran between her and the boy, trying to stare him back. "Don't touch her!" he shouted.

The boy only laughed at him.

"Stop laughing!" Qudra shouted. His face blossomed red.

The lead boy kicked Saya again in the belly. "What did you get? Answer me!"

"Nothing," she said. "We don't have anything."

The boy saw the stocking laying in her lap. He reached out and grabbed it, felt the coins inside it, weighing it in his hands. He smiled.

Saya shook. "No, you can't have that. That is our last chance. Please."

The boy signaled his companions to take the stockings held by her other students.

"Stop!" Aafi cried. "You can't have that. That's ours. We got it, not you."

The boy shoved him to the ground.

Saya wept in frustration. She felt buried beneath a mountain of anger and fear. She looked at all of her children, and saw the fear in their eyes, but also the determination, the focus.

Saya realized she did not need to save her children. She *already had* saved her children. She had taught them confidence and nurtured their abilities. They had become strong because of her. She had taught them that determination.

Tashim reached out. He liked to use his hands to guide his spheres, flicking with his fingers to help his mind move his marble-sized shapes them this way and that. He flicked his fingers at the boys. None hit, but they slammed into the wall of the building behind them, spraying dust and chips of stone.

One of the boys reached for a knife in the sheath at his belt, but suddenly Aafi was staring at him. When the boy tugged on the hilt, it did not come free. He struggled with it, yanking with all his might but it did not budge. Saya smiled through the tears in her eyes. Aafi had increased the friction of the sheath acting on the blade until it was stronger than the boy's arm could overcome.

Another boy lunged at Aafi, but Faloush wove a wall before him, a flat plane. It was the largest he had ever made, though it was only two feet square, but he put enough mass into it that the boy caught it with his hip as if he had run headlong into a stone. He spun and flopped onto the ground, eyes wide.

The boy who had kicked her lurched into a rage all over again. He grabbed Saya by the throat. He lifted her to her feet and slammed her into the wall, choking her. Her face went numb, her lips rubbery. Her eyes bulged out. Her lungs screamed for air, but he held her tight.

She glimpsed Tashim over his shoulder. The boy held up both fists. His hands flashed open, and his body shook and a dozen tiny spheres lanced through the air, so many that Saya could actually see the air distorting around them. They flew above her head, slamming into the boy who held her, piercing him like arrows, bursting out the other side of his body. Blood sprayed onto the wall, onto the street, and onto Saya's robes.

The boy crumpled. Dead.

The other boys dropped the stockings and fled screaming.

Saya staggered back, steadying herself on the wall. She stared into the wide-open eyes of the dead boy, his choking hands now limp and lifeless. He was gone, but Saya did not feel relief. The air stank of burning oil. Visible afterglow floated everywhere, brushing against the walls, hissing out of the holes where the spheres had smackedflesh and stone.

Saya turned to Tashim. "What have you done?"

His whole body shook, mouth hanging open, eyes so wide they looked like they would never close again. Already the clouds of magick afterglow snaked around him, shimmering silver, drifting like glittering smoke from a starlight fire. It coated his hands and floated in the air about him.

The Priests would investigate word of a killing. The warren-bosses would surely call upon them to do so. They would come here and see Tashim's afterglow everywhere. They would be able to track it.

It killed her that she could not reach out to him, to hug him and tell him it would all be well. She could not risk any of his afterglow attaching to her clothes and skin. It was all she could do to hold her hands away when every bit of her heart was screaming at her to take the little boy in her arms and cocoon him in a soothing embrace.

She looked upon him sadly. *You cannot come home to the school until your afterglow has dissipated.* Her eyes filled with tears. She did not have the strength yet to say it out loud to him.

"Saya?" Qudra asked.

"I need to think," Saya said.

Sotta wept. "Can Tashim come home with us?"

Saya glanced at him. "No."

"Saya, what do we do?" Faloush asked, so agitated he bounced up and down on his heels.

Tashim could not come home. The stains of his magick would give away the location of the school, and every last one of them would burn. The Priests and their Glassdogs could use their tools on this afterglow to find him anywhere he went, no matter how fast he ran, or how well he hid. She realized he would not be safe anywhere. They could find him no matter where.

Her heart deflated when she realized she was looking at Tashim for the last time. As long as that afterglow remained here, he was doomed to be discovered.

Tashim turned his eyes to Saya, his body yet unable to move. "Saya, I want to go home."

"I am going to think of something," Saya promised him.

"Please, Saya," he pleaded. His face was ashen, his expression bleak.

"I will fix this," Saya told him. "I will find a way."

"But how?"

I do not know.

She looked up at the walls. They seemed a thousand feet high. She gazed down the alley, stretching in her mind until it went on for miles. They were trapped here in this moment, unable to escape.

As long as the afterglow stains remained, there was no chance.

As long as they *remained*.

But if she could prevent it from remaining here...

They could not outrun the afterglow, but they could face it head-on.

"We will clean this place," she said. "The way we clean ourselves. We must wipe away every trace. We must do this to protect Tashim."

The children all nodded as one.

"But Saya," Sotta said. "We have no crystal soaps."

She firmed her lips and nodded resolutely. "We must steal from the normals. Again."

12

A Cup Of Salt When You Are Thirsty

WHEN SAYA FIRST SET FOOT in the market, she knew she was going to steal.

She did not have time for any other way. She knew she would be burning bridges here. She could be recognized by shopkeeps, branded a thief. That would bring with it its own problems, but she would have to solve those problems when they came. She knew Terak would be disappointed in her, but for now she needed one thing, and one thing only.

Cleaning supplies.

Specifically, the kind that would most quickly wash away magick afterglow—ranum crystal powder, granulum crystal soaps, and obsidian sand. She had already dispatched Aafi, Qudra, and Sotta to three of their secret cleaning stations to bring the talcum, cloths, and pitchers of water. But they needed more than that to clear that much afterglow and sensitized fluorescence so quickly.

She was already exhausted before she even laid eyes on the shop she intended to rob. She knew Gahayan's two eldest boys would give chase. Saya was not sure she could outrun them at the best of times, let alone with an empty stomach and a broken sandal strap.

I cannot stop. I cannot give in. We are too close.

Saya had made it all her days without ever taking the life of another. She had schooled each of the children in the ways she had learned to hide and run so that they, too, would never have to find themselves in such a situation.

Now all that was shattered.

One of those sweet children had taken a life.

In front of witnesses.

With magick.

Now the part of her mind calculating the most stealthy route to pay Jacobas, and the part wondering if anyone would notice the theft at the Moneychanger before the afterglow died, and the part wondering when she next needed to order a bottle of Aafi's medicine, and the part wondering how she could ever look Noqer in the eyes again, were all being squeezed together and crushed by the fear that Tashim would never smile again and by the terror that the warren rats would bring the Priests to hunt him.

The urge to run was overwhelming, but she knew they could not. Not until they had cleaned the scene. Each of the places where the projectiles Tashim rendered made contact with any surface would be tainted with a splat of afterglow, as would his hands, and even the air around where he had stood. Every chip in the alley walls, every scrape of the stone street, even the wounds, where his tiny spheres had punctured clothing and flesh—all would be splashed with glowing paint, laced with a subtle hissing cloud, writhing tendrils of invisible smoke.

The Glasseyes could see them through their little lenses. And the Glassdogs who they forced to live behind those eyes were always on the streets. Always hunting.

Waiting for her outside were only Adrani and Faloush. Tashim was near catatonic. She could not possibly leave him alone like that. She left Mara with him, to hold the socks full of coins and watch the scene until she returned. The two boys would have to throw two or more grown men off her trail without using any more traceable magick.

I still have to make it to Jacobas before sunset. She began going over the stealthiest route but then worried the route might not be fast enough, so she thought of alternates, but the fastest routes were the most exposed, so she tried to order them in order of speed and difficulty, and then...

She slapped herself. Hard.

You are not there yet, Saya. She could not afford to think ahead. If she could not clear the scene of afterglow, the Priests could trace Tashim to wherever he chose to hide. If they found him, they could torture him or trick him into giving away the location of the school. Then it would not matter if she paid Jacobas or not.

And to keep Tashim safe she needed to clean the scene, and to clean the scene she needed the supplies, and to find the supplies she would have to steal from people she considered friends. Right here. Right now.

She stepped through the door and was confronted by a gauntlet of many tables, each stacked high with casks of half-sour springwine, stone plates, and mismatched sets of copper utensils. Gahayan's shop was deep, every wall lined with shelves of imported goods, some from thousands of miles away, imported by Mistine's Mercantile Empire.

This was a shop she knew well, yet had never been able to afford anything in. The meager supplies of ranum crystal powder and obsidian sand she had accumulated over the years had come from second-hand sources or bartered for with other thieves. The full bottles kept here cost half a year of the take from one of her students pickpocketing.

She did not belong here. And one look from Gahayan at his counter told her he knew it, too. He motioned to his sons before she was halfway to the back wall, where the bottles of expensive oils and powders sat.

She picked up the first bottle, and already she heard their footsteps behind her. She snatched up the second with ease, but the third, the obsidian sand, was on the top shelf, and even on tiptoes she could not reach. She put one foot on the lowest shelf, hugging the other bottles to her chest with one arm, and using the edge of the shelf above to pull herself up to grasp the last bottle. She teetered for a moment, but kept her balance and stepped off the shelf.

But her fear got the better of her. So many of her thoughts were wondering how close the shopkeep and his sons were, that she took her eyes off the ground before her heel touched down behind her. She glimpsed them threading the display tables, converging on her, but what she did not see was the woodrat claw talisman beneath her foot.

When she set her weight on it, the sharp sensation made her bend her leg. She turned her ankle and crashed backward into a table covered in wine bottles and mua dog carvings. One table leg snapped loose, and she dropped on her back beneath a hail of heavy wood and glass.

She closed her eyes and hugged the three bottles of soap as full bottles of wine fell like hammers on her arms, hips, and face, bruising, rolling off and shattering. A wet rush blossomed under her as the wine began to spread, soaking her robes. She opened her eyes and saw all three men looming over her, but one by one they slipped on shards of glass and wine and fell flat on their backs, making the floor quake.

Saya rolled upright. Tried to run. A strong hand clamped about her ankle. She forced herself upright, shaking herself free. Her sandal slipped and she dropped on her forearm. She heard a crunch of glass, raw pain streaking up her arm. Kicked to her feet and bolted. It felt like running in place at first, as wet as the floors were, kicking up broken glass and splashing red everywhere as she went.

At last she scampered out the door and into the street. Bright sun blasted her, forcing her arm up to cover her eyes. The heat sucked the breath out of her, her sandals scratching to a halt on white sand.

Saya was immediately conspicuous—back soaked red and gold, still dripping from her sleeves, her hair a shambles, shaking hands cradling three bottles which anyone with two eyes could plainly see were too expensive for her hands to be holding.

The street was wide here, much of it annexed by the poormarkets, row upon row of low square tables beneath canvas, where the scumborn peddled their wares. Every pair of eyes turned to look. Strangers she could handle, but it was the disappointed eyes of the shopkeeps who had helped her in the past that stung the most. She wondered how long it would take to ever earn their trust again. Maybe forever.

She finally caught a breath and pulled it in, fighting against heat and fear until her lungs were full. She tried to walk at first, calm and quiet, but she made it no more than halfway across before she heard Gahayan shouting.

"Stop her! Stop her! Thief!"

The word was like a knife through her heart, killing her over and over again.

She took off at a run, dodging people, leaping over pushbrooms, jumping and spinning away from reaching arms, and using the tables for cover.

She nearly made it to the other side before a stone struck her head. It did not hurt so much, but it dazed. Her eyes fogged over, her vision splitting, losing focus. What she thought to be the entrance of a narrow alley turned out to be a pale stone wall.

Her forehead smacked it first and then her wrists and then her knee. The impact jolted her back. She teetered, fell forward, landed on her elbows, rolled. Through it all she hugged tight the bottles.

She felt heavy hands on her shoulders, spinning her around. It was one of Gahayan's sons. Thick fingers closed over her wrists, trying to pry them apart to take the bottles from her.

But Adrani was suddenly beside her. She held a ripe calpas fruit in her hand, plundered from a nearby cart. She tossed it to the man, forcing him to let Saya go so he could cover his face. Just then, Faloush swung a broken table leg into the side of his head. Faloush may have been a small boy, but his aim was true. The end smacked Gahayan's son just behind the eyes and he dropped like a stone.

Saya pushed herself up, fighting through the pain. She saw broken glass sticking out of her arm. She wanted to scream at the sight of it, but she choked it back down.

She noticed Faloush raise his hands. A miniature cloud of glittering particles slithered about his hands.

He is binding streams!

She swatted him across the face. "No!" she cried. "Not here!"

He cupped his cheek. "But I—"

"Just go!" she cried.

She swung Faloush by his collar, dragging him behind her as she ran down the narrow street, kicking up a cloud of white dust as she ran. They took many turns before Saya dared let them stop to catch their breaths in a long, narrow alley.

The air was so hot it had weight, threatening to flatten her to the ground. She felt like she was trying to pull every breath through a burlap bag. Her arms and legs were so sore she was afraid to sit down, lest she never rise again.

She turned on Faloush. She pointed at the glittering stains on his hands. "I told you, no magick. What were you thinking?"

"Sorry, Sayani," he said. "It is fading already."

"It remains there invisible even after it fades to our eyes. How many times have I explained this to you? The hunters can see it with their lenses. If one of them looked at you right now they would see it plain. You must be more careful. The whole reason we are doing this is to hide Tashim's afterglow, and here you are, bumbling in his footsteps."

He looked like he was about to cry. "I'm sorry, Sayani. Swear to Juna that I am."

Her shoulders sagged. She felt a fool for yelling. "Please be more careful."

He nodded. "I understand."

She glanced up. Saw a man at the end of the alley, staring at her. Her heart jumped. His hair was fifty shades too light to be a native, and he wore a tunic fifty shades too dark for the Kasaban sun.

He took a step toward her.

No, please. Not now. Not again.

She kept her eyes on him. Keeping so still. Eyes wide. She pressed the jars of soaps into the hands of the children, and guided them behind her, spread her arms, hands open flat, backing them away. They knew her mind. Adrani and Faloush were good students. They huddled silently behind her.

The man kept coming, until he was only five paces from her. He glanced over his shoulder, then looked at the air before Faloush.

She stared fiercely at him. *He knows.*

He should not have been able to see the afterglow. It was already invisible even to Saya. But he must have known somehow. He had the look of a hunter.

He stood a head taller than she, tunic molded to his body by the heat of morning, boots new to the desert, black leather still clinging to its original color, not yet stained white from the endless desert dust.

The sight of him struck her, the same way she felt the first time she laid eyes on Khersas. His stare held her still, as if her body was on the end of a string he pulled, drawing her toward his arms, slender, wired with muscle, his stomach flat as the endless basin of the desert. Face blank, cheeks shrouded with stubble, hair unruly and wild, mouth dry, gaze hungry, his eyes sharp enough she wondered if they had drawn her blood just by looking at her. His gaze was sympathetic, but his lip curled with a hidden anger, as if a part of him hated her even though they had never before met.

She backed away, turned her head down. Fear climbed up her tongue, making her feel hollow.

He took another step. "Afterglow," he said. "Dangerous."

She narrowly avoided choking on her tongue. She knew in that moment that he was just as capable of giving her all she asked and taking away everything she held dear. She glanced urgently down either way of the narrow street, searching every door and window for a route to get the children away from him.

He took a step back, still watching her. He held up both hands, palms out. He then pointed at the air in front of her. "If one of them looks with the lens, they will see."

How does he know?

She kept still, realizing she had fallen into a trap with no way out. The children gawked at him, sniffling meekly.

He held up his open hands. "I won't hurt you. I won't tell anyone."

I do not believe you. I cannot believe you. She shook her head at him. *You can say that until it snows in Kasaban.* "Such a promise is a mirage."

That was when she noticed the Priest walk past the other end of the street, bright white crusading robes unmistakable, stopping, turning a gold mask to look down the alley at her.

Another man joined the Priest, dressed in brown wool trousers and a sky-blue shirt with sleeves rolled up, and matching headband. He stood beside the Priest and fished a monocle from his pocket.

The sight of him made Saya's legs wobble. She did not know how she remained on her feet.

Glasseye.

The stranger directly in front of her responded to the appearance of the Priests by reaching into his carry-bag and withdrawing a slender grey stick. He struck it with his thumbnail. It shined like the sun itself had been born in his hand. Her eyes turned away from it, holding one hand up to shield them.

He waved it in the air, dancing from one foot to the other, hopping to an imaginary rhythm. Saya thought he had gone mad before her eyes, but at the far end of the alley, the Glasseye lowered his lens and shook his head at the Priest. They both walked on.

The bright light died out.

The relief rolled over her until she was a hairsbreadth from passing out.

The stranger tossed the stick to the ground. "The lens lets them see, but they still need eyes to look through it. Blind the eyes and it doesn't matter what the lens reveals."

She nodded. What did he want from her? That was the question. Jacobas had taught her that no one did anything for free in Kasaban. She waited for him to make his demands.

"My name is Aren," he said. "What is yours?"

She looked at him closely. "No one."

He tilted his head and peered around her. "Are you their mother?"

"No," she said. "Teacher." *Why did you say that to him? You fool. The school must be a secret. The teacher must be a mystery.*

"You...teach them? To render?"

She narrowed her eyes at him. His naivety made her bite her lip at the unfairness of the world. That anyone could live in this world and not know the fear and anguish that followed the magi of her city every moment of their lives was too much to bear.

"Thank you for what you have done, but now please go away." She had the coin to pay Jacobas and half a year besides. She had the soaps to clean up after Tashim. She would not risk owing any favors. She knew Kasaban too well for that.

"We could help you."

"This is the place we know. Your boots have never walked a day in Kasaban sand. I see no tears on your cheeks and I see the light of hope still shining behind your eyes. You do not know Kasaban. You have no idea what harm you can do here."

He recoiled. "No tricks. I promise."

"A promise is as worthless as a cup of salt when you are thirsty," she said. "A promise means nothing in this place."

She thought of Tashim and Mara waiting for her and winced.

I do not have time for this.

She turned her back on the stranger, gathered her students behind her, and moved on to the next street, making sure he did not follow before they turned the corner. She learned long ago that promises were best left behind, like footprints in the sand.

Saya wound her way through the city with her students, like water coursing through narrow white ravines. Every moment it took to get there was another moment closer to them all being cast into the fires. Every time she blinked she saw the gold mask of Sevastin Karda looming over her, or the crazed crystal eyes of the Glassdog, teeth bared like an animal as he chased her. They would be waiting for the children, too, if she did not hurry.

Her feet ached from walking, yet she could not remember taking a single step all that way. All she remembered were the white walls passing by her, faster and faster, until she blinked and she was there.

Instead of seeing Mara and Tashim waiting, she was greeted with a fresh new horror. The warren gang had returned with a smallboss. All five of them wandered about the alley, barefoot, blue vests over ivory tunics and trousers, ears pierced with desert rat fangs. The smallboss wore a coat with a torn sleeve and a red cap. They revolved about the scene, clearly not wanting to be here but unsure what to do, peering at the body, dancing on tiptoes around the puddle of blood.

Oh Juna, are we too late?

A hand wrapped around her mouth, and a voice whispered in her ear. "Hush now." It was Mara. She had Tashim and Noqer in tow.

Saya nodded. "What has happened?"

"They have not touched the body yet," Mara said. "Or any of the chips in the walls."

Saya noticed none of them were the same boys that ran away. "What are they doing?" Saya asked.

"The ones who were here before did not come back," Mara said. "They must have told the tale, and now these ones came to check on it."

"They look like they are trying to convince each other it was magick," Adrani said.

"They are," Noqer whispered, his lips uncomfortably close to her ear. "They do not believe the tale of their youngers."

"They do not want to believe," Saya said. "They are as afraid to call the Priests as we are."

"They will not call the Priests," Noqer said.

Saya turned to him. His eyes looked right through her, like he was a different boy than the one she knew. "Why do you sound so sure?"

Noqer smiled. "I fixed it."

She narrowed her brow. "What do you mean you fixed it?"

"I took care of it. The way a man does." He smiled at Saya and then at Adrani, in a way that was both satisfied and demanding.

Saya turned to Mara for an explanation.

"He carved the symbol of a rival warren gang onto the neck of the dead boy."

Saya could barely contain a gasp. "You sullied the dead?" Holy Juna would be none too pleased at the violation of her sacred law. "That is desecration. That is what the Priests do."

Noqer shrugged as easily as if he had stolen a pastry. "I did it for you. For us. He did not seem to mind."

"But to deface the dead..." Saya lost her words.

"He was warren scum," Noqer said. "He deserved it."

"No one ever deserves it," Saya said.

Noqer smirked. He had never made such a dismissive face before. It both startled and saddened her. "I say he did deserve it. For laying bad hands upon you."

"Look," Adrani said. "They are leaving on their own."

"Going to fetch the warren boss," Mara said. "To show him the symbol."

"They will not even move the body until the warren boss sees," Noqer said.

"That means we have not a moment to waste," Saya said. "We must clean this place before they return."

They raced about to find every point where one of Tashim's projectiles struck an object. The other children arrived with the cloths and water soon after. Saya unstoppered the bottles of crystal soaps and they set to work. Mara ruthlessly tracked down every chip in the walls, every crack in the street, and Aafi, Sotta, and Faloush wet them and scrubbed them until their fingers were raw.

While they worked on the walls, Saya dragged the body to the edge of the blood puddle and poured the soaps and powders over every wound. She averted her eyes as she scrubbed, swearing to Holy Juna that she was only cleaning the corpse, not harming it. The skin was still warm. More than once the mouth would give up a hiss, and each time she panicked, thinking somehow the boy was still alive.

She did not let the others stop until she was certain every trace of afterglow had been dissolved. By then the sun was hanging low on the horizon.

She tried to draw their attention away from the body as much as she could. She kept them distracted by handing each one a sock full of coins and an empty bottle or pitcher to carry home. She was already shaking, head swimming, stomach growling, feet aflame, but she still made them all follow her through the hidden paths and secret spaces to a hiding spot, where they could each wash themselves up once more. Just to be sure.

Saya stripped down and bathed herself by splashing water from the basin Radir had left there for them. She forced the other children to do the same, scrubbing with lye and a stiff-bristled brush. She set a small fire in the middle of the empty room and burned copious amounts of rosewood, until the smoke nearly choked her. She ruffled her hair, letting the smoke wash over her, then she burnt all of their clothes, and doused the flames with what water remained in the basin. They all dressed in fresh clothes left for them by Radir.

When they finally poured themselves through the sewer tunnels and arrived at the grate, Saya looked up at the light and saw high branches overhead. She allowed herself a smile, as each of the children handed her one of the socks full of coins and worked their way up into the safe grotto between four red brick walls.

Her smile flattened when she realized how dark it was getting. She felt the weight of the coins in her hand and felt the familiar fear creep back into her bones. She had forgotten about Jacobas. She had to deliver the coin to him today.

I have to get this money to Jacobas before nightfall or it was all for nothing.

She ran back through the tunnels, coins jingling, echoes ringing in her ears like a host of bells. She scampered through the back alleys of the city once more, winding her way to the warren-boss compound where Jacobas and the other warren scum of her cityside congregated.

She looked across the open courtyard but could not see him. *Already inside. Aya Jaytat.* She needed to make it inside to find him, without any of the others knowing. If they found out he was skimming a secret fee it would be the end for them both.

She took a deep breath, waved her hands in little focus-inducing spirals, easing her mind into the source, subtly binding her streams, and finally rendered an ovoid bubble of lightbending about herself, tethered to her body so that it would follow her without conscious direction. A brief shimmer of silver and violet shivered across her hands, crawling up her wrists like smoke, dissipating into the air like steam. She knew the stains were still there, invisible. She would need to avoid touching anything on her way in or out.

The last arc of the sun was dipping out of sight. *You can do this.*

She crossed the open courtyard and ducked into a narrow, sagging doorway. Everything was dark wood, old, crumbling, patched and repaired a hundred times over. Everything smelled of musk and roasting meats and old wine. She snaked her way through the corridors, careful to never pass too close to another, lest her bubble pass over them and they realize something was amiss.

She neither brushed her shoulders against a wall, nor touched a door handle, fearful she might smear the afterglow that gathered on her hands every time she rendered magick. She made it all the way to the private rooms, where she found Jacobas with a street woman, one who was much better at pretending to enjoy it than she was.

She stepped into the room and changed the stream of duration in her bind to nothing, and the bubble winked out of reality. The sudden sight of her panicked Jacobas and he tumbled over backwards, trousers about his ankles, knocking the poor woman onto the floor.

"Where did you come from?" he asked angrily.

"I have the money," she said.

"Next time announce yourself," he grumbled, hitching up his pants, and sending the street woman on her way.

"I have your fee," she said.

His eyes lit up. "Here?"

She dumped out the contents of three of the socks into his waiting palms. "It is all there," she said. "As you asked."

He grinned greedily, licking his lips. "You have surprised even me. The deal stands. You have your home another cycle."

Saya teared up with relief.

She barely made it.

But she made it.

Thank you, Holy Juna.

She exited the compound just as carefully, touching nothing, pretending to be a poor servant. She fooled everyone. They were too focused on their supper and their street women to notice her.

She wound her way home, careful she was not followed, stopping at a secret cleaning site only she knew of, in the basement of a bricked-up abandoned home, where the only access was a narrow hole in the side of a dried-up well.

She peeled herself out of her stained and torn robes, and washed herself aggressively, scrubbing her skin with the bristly brush, using the little dab of crystal soap she found there. She scattered talcum powder and rinsed with water again. She changed into the clean set of robes she had left here years ago, untouched all this time.

She stumbled home, using a torch to make it through the tunnels, banging on the underside of the grate until Radir came to open it and give her a hand up. He smiled gladly, and she let her forehead fall until it touched his. She pulled away and nodded. No words were needed.

She wanted to collapse, but of course, it was time for supper, so she set herself to making sure each of the children had enough to eat, then settled Tashim into his room, embracing him until he fell asleep, and then patiently explaining to each of the others why they must never speak of it again, especially not where Tashim could hear. By then the meal was stale and cold. She ate it anyway.

Her joints were grinding, her muscles burning, every inch of her aching for the sweet release of collapsing into her bed, burrowing into her blanket, nesting among her pillows. But it took until midnight before she could get the last of the children to sleep.

When she finally made it to her room, she did not even have the joy of feeling herself drift to sleep. She simply dropped onto the bed and her eyes went black.

13

Masks Of Gold

SAYA CLOSED HER EYES and thought back to the day before, going over the escape again and again, trying to remember every detail, to make sure she had forgotten nothing. She knew that such a brazen theft would surely arouse some activity among the Glasseyes, and then if any of them found the body...

She judged that it was best if she was thrice careful. She could not think of a single detail she had missed. Her home was preserved, her stability assured, high walls protecting them from all the dangers of the world. A place where they knew every street and every shop and every place to hide. Leaving it was unthinkable.

She returned to her memory of the stranger. She had little time to wonder much about him, but now her curiosity had time to flourish. He had thrown the Glassdogs off her scent, so he certainly was not one of them. She supposed it did not matter. He was just another northerner who knew nothing of Kasaban. What was his promise worth?

Saya was sick and tired of promises. Her mother and father had promised her that everything would be all right. Khersas had promised he would never leave her.

A promise is as worthless as a cup of salt when you are thirsty. All that matters is what you have and what you can buy and what you can take.

She had enough to worry about without clouding her thoughts with any of that. Tashim had not come out of his room and it was nearly noon. Serine was anxious to try another sphere, but she wanted Tashim to be there to see how well she was doing. She had asked after him twice already and even gone to knock on the door to his room, but he had not answered.

Saya sorely needed a simple teaching session with her students in the yard, surrounded by their four safe red brick walls.

Is it too much to ask to leave yesterday in the past and never speak of it again?

"Did Tashim truly kill someone?" Tana immediately asked.

Saya shook her head.

It was too much to ask.

Lili gasped, despite the fact that she already knew it to be true.

"Tashim is ashamed," Qudra said. "He took life, and now he has to pray for forgiveness. Holy Juna says so."

"Why?" Raba asked. "He was protecting Sayani. It was the right thing to do. Noqer says so."

"Noqer has no gods," Qudra said. "The gods of my father require prayer if you take a life."

"What do your gods know?" Raba demanded, leaping up and shoving Qudra. "Where did your gods run to when your father died? Holy Juna is the goddess of weaklings."

Qudra slapped him before Saya could get between them. "The Priests burned my father!" Qudra shouted.

"And your gods hid under the bed, just like you did," Raba taunted, scratching at Qudra's face.

Saya first tried to bear-hug Raba. He was the smaller of the two, but his arms were locked with Qudra's in a grapple, and when she made to pull him away, her arms slipped off him. She reached between them and pushed them apart. She grabbed hold of each of their wrists and stared hard at them, furious.

"There will be none of that," she said. "You shame me by fighting in our school. You two need each other. We all need each other, and Tashim needs us. We are stronger together. That is what this place is. We look out for each other. We give each other strength when we can. We take strength when we need it. That is what it means to be a family. You should both be giving your strength to help Tashim. I will not have you fighting like this. The Priests come for children who fight."

Raba's struggles finally died down and he huffed angrily. When Saya released him, he folded his arms across his chest and scowled.

Qudra just walked away, slamming the front door of the main house and stomping up the stairs to where Adrani was practicing her buoyancy renders in the brass tub.

Saya sighed. "Raba, go stand in the corner by the willow tree until I say."

"But..." Raba protested. "That's not fair. Qudra just..."

"Go now!" Saya said. "I will deal with Qudra, but there is no fighting permitted and you know it, as you know you should not have said those hurtful things to Qudra." She stared at him severely until he went to stand beneath the willow, pouting.

Saya turned back to the girls—Tana, Lili, and now Serine, who had joined them after hearing the commotion. They all looked awkwardly at her, terrified and curious. "Raba and Qudra are just upset over what happened, and because Tashim has not come out today. Sometimes boys act out when they are worried or frightened, but we must not be cross with each other no matter how we feel. We are all a family here, aren't we?"

All three girls nodded enthusiastically.

"Good, now where were we today? Are you going to practice making two-dimensional planes today, Tana?"

Tana nodded, equally enthusiastically.

"And you, Lili? Are you going to try to make water flow through the piece of wood again?"

Lili shook her head. "I made water go through that board yesterday," she said, exasperated, as if it was old news she had been forced to repeat a dozen times already.

"Well, we will have to get you a thicker board to try then," Saya said. "Why don't you run around to the side of the house and bring me one of those fat fence posts?"

Lili was up and running before Saya could blink.

"What about you, Serine?"

Serine folded her arms and looked away. "I will not make a sphere until Tashim can come see."

Saya smiled. Serine's small grimace was as adorable as it was stubborn. "Let's see if we can convince him to come out and see. What do you say?"

Serine eyed her suspiciously for a moment, but then nodded furiously, her eyes lighting up as if Saya had offered her a chocolate pie. Serine trotted toward the house.

Saya rose on stiff legs to follow her. She winced as the muscles of her abdomen tightened. The cuts on her arms throbbed angrily, and her bruised hip made her limp. She kept all her wounds well-covered with her robe. She did not want any of the children to worry about her. She did not even mind the pain. It was a small price to pay for all that she had gained.

She looked around at the yard—the main house and the poplar, the willow and the cedars, the ruined house, the shed, and the orange tree. The sparrows burst up into the air all at once, taking flight in a great flock, swirling around each other before fluttering off and dispersing. It was a beautiful aerial ballet. Saya watched with wonder. She took a deep breath of orange blossoms and smiled to herself. She loved the smell so much, just as her mother had, such a rare treat to have in Kasaban. Saya felt greedy. She took another deep breath, wishing to fill her nostrils with an endless parade of orange and cedar.

But when she took the second breath, she no longer smelled the orange blossoms. Or the cedar. She did not smell the dirt that had worked its way into the bricks. She did not smell the old wood of the house.

She smelled something strange, something foul, something that wafted in and fell atop the other smells, shoving them down, drowning them in a wave of rotten burning stench.

Saya looked all around. She spun, eyes searching frantically. At the tops of the high walls, at the trees, at the windows and doors of the main house and the ruined house. There was no smoke and no spill. She couldn't see anything at all, and yet the pungent smell persisted.

Something was horribly wrong. Her first thought was of where her students were, and how she might be able to gather them all. She was not sure why she thought of that.

Then she heard a sound.

It came from the center of the high wall across the yard from the orange tree, where they had long ago bricked up the entrance. Something was grinding against it, cracking the mortar, splitting the carefully stacked red bricks, sending twisting cascades of clay dust drifting down to the ground.

Saya stared at it.

She realized too late she should have been running.

The wall exploded inward with a thunderous crack. A brick sailed past her head. Another glanced off her knee, sending her to the ground. The center of the wall collapsed into rubble, drowning her in a cloud of dust so thick it hung in the air like fog. It coated her skin and clung to her teeth. She sucked a breath and choked violently on it.

She could barely see ten feet in front of her. She could only discern the outlines of the houses and trees, fallen bricks and crumbling mortar. And behind it all an enormous gap opened in the wall, exposing her home to the street outside.

My wall. In an instant, destroyed.

She saw the shadow shape of a man standing amid the rubble, framed perfectly by the trough of the collapsed wall. He stood so still, so horrifyingly calm, at peace amid the wreckage. She noticed a glint of light reflecting off his face, something catching the light. Something metal. Something gold.

Priest.

14

We Will Go Far Away Someday

THREE PRIESTS STEPPED THROUGH the rubble of the shattered wall, calmly surveying the yard. The number made no difference. If one knew of this place, then they all did.

Their golden masks hovered in the dust cloud, the yawning mouth holes screaming at her. They drifted forward like apparitions in white robes, arms at their sides, with a calm born of invincibility.

The first Priest said but one word. "Teacher." The mask he wore had etched into it a single tear beside one of the eyeholes.

Saya recognized that mark.

Burner of children.

It was Sevastin Karda. The White Death of Kasaban had come himself to claim his prize.

And with his Priests came a Glassdog, eyes forever imprisoned behind crystal lenses in leather goggles, lips peeled back around teeth that never stopped their furious clenching, hair slicked back into spikes like shards of onyx. His head never stopped moving, jumping this way and that, like a manic bird.

Saya's mind flew in a hundred different directions, thoughts diffusing into the air like dust.

Where are the children?

Serine was behind her. Or was she in the house? She tried desperately to remember. Raba beneath the willow, Faloush on the porch, Radir in his shed, Tana alone and terrified beneath a cedar, Tashim, Adrani, Qudra, and Noqer somewhere in the house.

Her mind shattered trying to think of a way to gather them all and flee with them through the drain into the sewers. But the hidden grate sat in the center of the yard, directly in front of the Priests.

Who had used magick where and how recently? What could the Priests see? Who could they track? *Can we even escape? Or can they follow our trail?*

Radir emerged from his shed. The door to the main house creaked, Tashim poking his head out, eyes like saucers. Noqer followed behind him, stunned, confused.

The students must have all been covered with the stains of magick from the way the Glasseye reacted to them. Of course they were. They never washed them off when safe at home. There had never been a need.

The Glasseye backed away, taking the Priest by the sleeve of his white robe, and gesturing at them all.

Sevastin Karda shrugged out of his grip, ignoring the warning.

How did they find us? Her mind raced, trying to think of what she had done wrong, how she had failed. They had washed and cleaned everything.

She noticed one of the Priests dragging someone else along, fingers clamped about the back of their neck, wrangling them like a misbehaving child. They were thrown to their knees out in front of the Priests.

It was Jacobas.

He groaned and clutched at his stomach. His face was bloodied, and when he winced Saya could see many of his teeth missing. Through all the blood she could barely make out a nose or a mouth. He huddled there, crying like a child, blood dripping out his nose and eyes.

Saya clutched at her heart. Horror turned her knees to straw. Her stomach plummeted through the ground to the center of the earth.

This can't be happening. This isn't happening. This can't be happening.

One of the Priests forced Jacobas upright on his knees, and spread out his hands, shoulder-width apart. The Glassdog studied them through his crystal goggles. And then he turned and stared through his awful glass eyes at Saya. The Glassdog pointed at her.

She had made a mistake. She realized it with agonizing clarity. It was one small mistake, a little thing, a tiny thing after all these years of vigilance, but it was enough to erase every single time she had ever been careful before, all the caution she had practiced and acted out her whole life.

She realized she had used magick to make herself invisible to sneak past the warren-boss and his kin to find Jacobas in time to pay. When she had returned from paying Jacobas, she had remembered to change her clothes and wash herself and take the longest path home. She knew she had to remove those stains of magick from herself. Just as they all had after escaping the Moneychanger. She had banished every puff of invisible smoke, and washed away every hint of sensitized fluorescence from her hands and body.

She cleansed herself of afterglow to perfection.

But *Jacobas* had not.

She had touched nothing with her hands when seeking out Jacobas, holding tightly to the socks full of coins, the ones she had handed him to pay the fee he demanded. She had been so careful not to touch anything there.

But she had touched the socks. She had left the stain of her magick upon them when she used her hands to press the coins into his hands. They in turn passed it to him. She had sensitized his hands.

The Priests and their Glassdogs had been out in triple force searching for the afterglow of magick. One of them must have seen it on Jacobas while he was out spending the money Saya had paid him. The Priests could use their tools to trace such things back to their creator, triangulate her position, know precisely where she was relative to the stains of magick she had left behind.

In one careless moment, she had led them here.

She was undone.

Saya stood frozen, hoping beyond hope that if she was just still enough, she would wake from this nightmare. But it did not end.

Sevastin Karda's voice growled to life. "Consorting with the unholy is sin. Keeping secrets is sin. You have defied the Lord of Truth. You shall be hanged." He tapped Jacobas on the forehead to punctuate each statement. Jacobas cried out, and whimpered as a pair of Ministry acolytes dragged him out into the street.

It is my fault.

Saya's eyes were swollen. Her heart dropped out of her chest. She had been so full of joy that she had succeeded in finding the money, in setting their school up for life, that she had forgotten one little thing. And it cost her everything.

It is my fault.

Saya could not move.

You must move.

You must protect the children.

Sevastin Karda swirled his arms around in the air, spinning his hands. The air distorted with all the shapes he rendered. She felt them all pre-exist the instant before they became real. Spheres, like marbles, lightning fast. So many. Dozens at once. The concentration to do that...

He is like a god next to us.

We have to get out of here. Now.

"Abominations," Karda said. He rendered a cube about Noqer, locking him in place. He slammed his palms at invisible sides, and stomped on an invisible bottom, trapped within.

His words set Saya into motion. She grabbed Serine up in her arms and ran under the posts of the ruined house, trying to blend into the shadows. Faloush bolted from the porch, running toward her.

She reached for the source, ready to bend the light around herself and Serine, and poor Tana, alone under the cedar tree.

But she couldn't. She strained her mind, feeling around for the streams she was looking for, what she needed, but they were not there. Something was stopping her.

They were stopping her.

She saw three men standing in the street outside her walls, unmoving, eyes ahead, locked in concentration. They stared at nothing. They did nothing. They only thought. *There they are.* Three Stoppers. Of course, they would have recorded the magick she had used to get to Jacobas. She had left a blueprint for how she constructed her invisibility lightbending renders when she left that afterglow behind. The Stoppers had it, and they had cut her off from those streams.

I need to render something else, something they have not seen.

Saya scrambled about within the Slipstream for her other streams, she found a series that she often bound together to create flat reflective planes. They were there for the taking.

She rendered six mirror planes, each as tall as herself, placing them in front of Tana and each of the boys, angled forty-five degrees to the Priests, replacing what they saw with the view of the wall and the trees. The reflections baffled the Priests, and allowed each of her students to duck, crawl, roll away from where they had been, their movements masked from Karda before he and his Priests could render cube cells about the others.

She placed the last in front of herself and Serine, reflecting light from the corner with the poplar tree. She thought it was a good idea until she saw Aafi standing beneath the poplar. He had been out of sight behind the corner of the main house until that moment. Saya had given him away.

But the Priests did not understand the angles. They rendered blank projectiles and sent them hurtling toward the reflected image of Aafi. Saya's mirror had no mass, so the spheres passed right through it, smacking into the side of the shed, and splintering the shutters of Radir's window.

Radir growled through gritted teeth in the doorway of his shed. He gazed out over Saya's head at the Priests across the yard. He rendered bubbles of heat about the three Priests.

The first heat bubble he bound the wrong *position* stream into, and it rendered over empty air, but the second one wrapped about one of the Priests. The heat rose so swiftly that the Priest was unable to jump free before his robes began to smoke. He tossed his golden mask to the ground, crawled out of the heat bubble, and rolled in the dirt to douse his blackened robes.

The third heat bubble enveloped Karda himself, but the White Death of Kasaban was faster than his brethren, feeling the ripples in the Slipstream a blink before Radir's render became real, giving him time to reflexively render a spherical bubble shield about himself. By the time the heat flared,

Karda was safe inside a sealed three-dimensional shell, that heat could not radiate through.

The Glassdog beside him was not so lucky. Locked outside the safety of Karda's shield, his clothes, hair, and skin burst into flames. He screeched like a mayda bird, the leather goggles melting to his face. He dropped onto his back screaming, the superheated crystal lenses sliding loose of their frames and dropping onto his eyes, making them sizzle in bursts of steam as they melted their way through his head to the back of his skull.

Karda left Noqer in his cube cell. The Priest could no longer see her other students through the mirrors, but he kept rendering spheres the size of his fist, hurling them at near the speed of sound, his arm movements becoming angrier, wilder. He threw them all over—in every direction— more and more mass contained within each one. She had thought he might run out of energy if she threw him off target enough times, but his renders just kept coming.

He rendered cubes in random locations, trying to trap more of the children, not caring if the rendered walls sliced any of their bodies in two if they appeared partway within.

Saya screamed at them all to get out of sight. She knew the Priests could not render outside of line of sight. It was impossible for any magi. Even Saya. But as the little ones hid themselves, Saya realized it would not matter. If they could not make it to the grate without being seen or cut apart, they would be found eventually. None of them were strong enough to overpower a Priest.

More invisible objects flew over her head, pelting the shed and the ruined house, cracking the beams and showering her with a haze of pulverized mortar. The posts holding up the roof of the porch snapped, and it sagged low, threatening to collapse in front of the door. The chair shattered. The bench turned to splinters. The front door was blasted apart.

The walls of the main house gave way like paper, every projectile punching holes through it and smashing apart the furniture within. The red brick walls chipped, circular spiderwebs of cracks radiating from the impact of every flying sphere.

Saya looked at the grate, hidden beneath canvas and leaves, then looked at where her students would be. They were all over. She was apart from them. She had no way to reach them and she needed to reach them, every one, leaving none behind, she had to keep them all safe and together with her forever.

One struck a cedar tree, splitting its trunk with a sharp snap, throwing Tana against the brick wall. She screamed, her hair matted with blood, spittle flying out as she shrieked.

Another flew into the upper floor of the main house, ripping the walls and roof apart as it burst, sending shards of glass and splinters and chips of stone shrieking across the courtyard. Pieces of beds and chairs poured out the gaps in the walls, plummeting to the yard below, landing with a rumble of thunder.

The explosion must have ruptured both of Adrani's oil lamps. A gout of flame shot in the air, splashing the inside walls, setting fire to her room and Saya's, their blankets erupting into a continuous smoke plume.

A piercing shriek sliced into her ears, peeling her hope away.

Among the debris, Saya saw two children on the ground. Adrani did not move at all, her skin blistered and blackened, her braid smoking, her slender eyes open forever. Qudra flopped around beside her, squealing, his limbs ablaze.

Saya screamed. Her mind could think of nothing else to do with the horror she saw.

She could not even put out the flames.

But Radir could. He bound streams and rendered a temperature decrease around Qudra. The flames shriveled without heat, the skin of Qudra's arms turning blue from the sudden cold. He rolled on the ground and moaned.

Saya flew to his side, her mirror panel shifting with her. She dropped and slid to a halt, skinning her knees in the dirt. Magick tore the world apart around her, gouts of debris pelting her, plumes of dirt blossoming into the air all around, trees breaking, wood snapping, bricks smashed to powder, every thunderous impact rattling her ears.

Yet it all slowed down for Qudra, time standing still in a little bubble around them both. Saya scooped him up in her arms, holding his head and shoulders in her lap. Both arms and half his face were charred crisp. It ripped tears from her eyes to see him in so much pain.

"Qudra, no, little one, no."

He reached one blackened hand to touch her face. "Sayani? Is that you?"

"It's me. I'm here. I've got you."

"It hurts, Sayani. It hurts."

"I know, little one. I know. It's going to be okay."

"I can't see."

"It's okay. I've got you."

"I'm sorry, Sayani. I'm sorry."

"Hush, Qudra. Don't be sorry, little one. I've got you."

"Please don't leave me, Sayani. I'm scared."

"I'm scared, too. But it's going to be okay because we're together."

"Promise?"

"Promise."

His little half-charred face curled into a smile. "Okay."

She wished she could carry him away and give him medicine and heal him until he was all better again, so that he could forever be the mischievous Qudra she loved so much.

But instead his little body died in her arms.

She did not even have the luxury to scream. All she could do was inch him off her lap and gently lay him in the dust.

Goodbye, Qudra. I'm so sorry I couldn't take you away from this.

Fire spread all through the main house, tongues of flames licking at the roof, smoke snaking out the windows. The pieces of the front door toppled and Sotta staggered out, stumbled, fell, rolled off the porch, a haze of smoke billowing out after him. Beni crawled behind him, coughing and crying, hands and face black with ash. Mara carried Timma out next. He wasn't moving at all in her arms.

At least the smoke blotted out the Priests. They tried to fan it away with magick, but it blessedly blotted out their vision, if only for a brief few moments.

Radir was focused on the flames in the main house, trying to draw heat away from it to keep it from becoming an inferno long enough for all the students to get away.

Saya thought of the year's worth of food and the lifetime of memories burning along with it. She looked down at Serine beside her. Tears were pouring out of her eyes. Tana was still screaming, blood flowing from the cedar splinters in her scalp. Sotta was stumbling and falling.

Why are you doing this to us? What have they ever done to you? Please stop. Please just go away. We will leave. We will go away. Please just stop.

Saya stood up. She could not save their home or their food, but she had to save the rest of the children. She had to. She had to stop this.

She looked at Tashim. Her good little boy. Who had been forced to grow up so far ahead of his time. "Throw your spheres now!"

Tashim obeyed her. He splayed out his fingers to aid his focus, and sent dozens of small spheres whistling at lightning speed across the yard.

Karda remained shielded, but the other Priests had not been expecting anything of this sort, and at least two of Tashim's spheres tore into them, blood blossoming into stains on their pure white robes.

Saya heard a sphere ping off of one of their gold masks, snapping the Priest's head back. The other was hit in the belly and pitched forward into the dirt, his face smacking down hard.

But Karda was still there before her, furious, binding streams, rendering death. The wind kicked up. The smoke was clearing. It had to be now.

Saya knew she only had one chance to get her children to safety, and she needed to bend light to do it. She needed to make the largest cocoon of invisibility she had ever made in her life, and those were the streams they were stopping her from using.

She stared at the three Stoppers out in the street, all so still, so focused. She knew about Stoppers. Khersas had taught her about them. They were each reaching into the Slipstream, touching *her own streams*, holding those she needed so that she could not reach them.

They need to be gone.

"Tashim!" she shouted. "Hit the men outside."

Tashim rendered spheres at them, but Karda must have heard. He rendered a flat shield in the way and all of Tashim's spheres smacked into it.

Saya needed another way.

"Sotta!" she cried. "Use a wave of air pressure! Out into the street! Now!"

Sotta obeyed without question. He sat up and threw his hands forward, and the air rippled as a wave of air pressure surged toward the Stoppers. It rippled the air around Kardas shields, and cascaded across the yard into the street. The wave hit the Stoppers like a mule kick, slamming them into a nearby wall and throwing them to the ground.

The Stoppers let go of her streams.

Saya reached into the limitless possibility of the source, awash in all the streams that had been denied her. She rendered an ovoid bubble, binding a stream to tether it to her, so it would move wherever she did. Light bent around her, and she became invisible to anyone outside its bounds. Priests stood directly in front of her, not ten paces distant, yet they looked right through her.

She rendered another around Radir, and one about Tashim, another about Sotta.

Saya took Serine by the hand and walked to each of the other students, motioning for them to come to her, gathering them up behind her. She swapped new streams of *size* into her bind structure as she went, widening the cocoon of bent light to accommodate each new child as she went.

The smoke was clearing. They had to go now. The children cried out. Their hands were all around her, trying desperately to hold on, trying desperately to make it.

She moved to the grate, her bubble obscuring its existence from the Priests, as Tashim sent another barrage of spheres over her head, and Radir wrapped them in heat so that they could not let their shields down for an instant without turning to ash.

She felt the drain grate with her hands and tore the canvas off. She wrenched the grate free as if it was made of straw and flung it aside. She pushed her students into the drain and down the rope ladder, first Raba and Serine, then Aafi then Faloush. She slowed to help Mara lower Timma down to the others. Sotta clambered down next, and then Tana. She sent Mara down and handed little Beni to her.

Saya sat on the lip of the drain. She looked up at the hazy patches of distorted light that hid Radir and Tashim.

"Radir! Tashim! Come now!"

Karda slowed. He studied the space behind Saya, near the tree beside Radir's shed. She thought it a blessing at first that he stopped punching wildly with his magick, until she realized he was staring coldly at the place where he had seen Tashim's spheres come from.

In his fury, Karda rendered a massive sphere at Tashim. Saya could not see it but she could see the air ripple around it. It shattered the front and snapped Tashim's ribs with a staccato crack, caving in his chest, and casting his blood upon the wall behind him. He spit up blood and tipped over forward, landing on his face as the shed collapsed atop him, a flurry of leaves cascading down on it.

Saya closed her eyes. She knew if she looked at his body, she would break down, she would fail. She did not have time to be hopeless just yet.

Saya took Lili under one arm, and began to lower herself down the rope ladder, carrying the girl under one arm.

Radir stepped up to the drain above her, the toes of his boots sticking out over the edge, his face high above, gazing down on her like a god.

Saya looked up at him as she dangled there, one hand on the rope ladder, gently swaying. "Please come, Radir! Hurry!" She did not know how much longer she could maintain the cocoon of invisibility around the drain. He had to come now.

Radir bent down, looked into her eyes and smiled. He did not climb down after her. "You are only weak right now," he said. "Not forever."

"Radir, what are you doing?"

"Leave now, come back stronger, fight again when you can win."

"Radir, please!"

He just smiled and slid the grate back over the drain. He nodded through the bars at her. "Don't forget," he said. "No matter how bad today is, there is always a chance tomorrow will be better."

Saya could not speak. She could not move. Tears leaked out the corners of her eyes.

Radir began binding streams into a myriad of useless renders in the air above the grate, so many that their afterglow was visible to the naked eye.

Saya understood what he was doing. He was creating so much of his own afterglow in the air above the drain that it would obscure Saya's, preventing the Priests and their Glasseyes from realizing the direction she and the children were heading for a few precious minutes.

Saya sniffled and sobbed and shook. She knew she would soon no longer be able to maintain the light-bending bubble around the drain.

Radir waved to her and pulled the canvas back over the grate, blotting out the sunlight. She heard him brush the leaves over the canvas to hide it.

When she reached the bottom of the ladder, she heard Radir scream, then cough twice, then scream again.

Saya stared at the grate above, submerged in the darkness of the tunnels, horror lurking just on the other side. She could not make herself stop looking. Her eyes shed more tears in that tunnel than all the raindrops that had ever fallen upon Kasaban. She wanted to cry herself to death just so that she did not have to feel it any longer.

The good thing about tomorrows is that there always is one.

Only not for all of us.

She felt a tugging at her sleeve. She looked down, eyes glazed, like a stunned rabbit. It was little Serine looking up at her, eyes barely visible in the dark.

"What do we do?" Serine asked, sniffling, wiping her nose with one sleeve.

"It is time to leave," Saya said. She had to be calm for them, for her children, so that they could go on.

There would be time later to stop and think and feel. A lifetime. Now was not the time for any of that. Now there was only time to leave the home she had built with her own hands. To leave home forever.

15

The Thing About Tomorrows

IN THE TUNNELS darkness was both friend and enemy.

Saya could not see where her feet touched down. She could not know for certain that the path ahead would be safe. She could barely keep all the children in sight when she looked over her shoulder. Light from the drains was pitiful, barely enough to see three steps in front of her. She tripped over bottles and boxes. She stepped on rats. She stumbled through dung. She sloshed through puddles that stank like they had been there for a thousand years.

But the hunters could not see her either. They were just as blind. More so even. For they did not know these tunnels. The Glasseyes. The soldiers. The Priests. They did not know which of them dead-ended, which ones linked to one another, and which ones secretly turned back on themselves. They did not know which grates gave way and led to the streets outside and which were rusted in place so that not even the strongest man could snap them loose.

The echoes were against pursuit, for so many of the tunnels in the ancient sewer system of Kasaban branched and diverged and interlinked that sounds seemed to come from every which way. Even now, the sound of men in the tunnels behind her came to Saya's ears in echoes from in front of her. An untrained tunnel runner would think them evidence of danger ahead. But Saya knew it was only phantoms.

Even though the children tried to be stealthy, they could not hope to be perfectly quiet. Aafi fell down more than once. Lili managed to kick every bottle they passed. Timma seemed to splash through every puddle of stagnant water. Raba's feet touched down so hard even when he tiptoed, that it sounded like the crack of a whip.

"Sayani, where are we going?" Lili asked, her whine as bad as a rusty gate.

"Hush," she snapped. "Be silent. They can hear."

"I've never been here," Lili protested. "I'm scared."

"No need to be scared of what is ahead," Saya said. "Because we are going there together."

That seemed to mollify Lili, but all the same, Saya did not know where she was taking them. The school—their home—had been everything. The hidden spaces where they stopped to wash after street runs were not suitable for living. Most could not even fit this many children at one time.

They could not be around normals. The little ones were not disciplined enough. They had lived so long without needing to suppress their powers at home. One of them would slip, and then it would all be over.

She knew in her heart they would have to leave the city. Kasaban without four safe walls to shield them from the rest of its horrors was just a hell of white sand and baking heat, gold masks and burning flesh.

But where could they go? And how could they get there? The nearest city was many leagues across open desert, and the roads were clogged, and infested with informants.

She needed guidance. She needed hope. She needed a divine light.

I will go to the temple of Holy Juna.

It was the one place in the city where the Priests did not hold sway. It was a place she could stop, if but for a short time until she found a way to escape this hell.

She turned to her students. "I know where to go."

As soon as she said the words, she saw him.

A Glasseye rounded the corner of a connecting tunnel. He was but a shadow of a man in the darkness, but he had one of the lenses held to his eye. With the lens he did not need to see her, he only needed to see the afterglow shedding from her hands, glowing on her sleeves, and her face, and her hair where she pulled it back as she ran. It was invisible to her, but it would shine like a beacon to him.

Her students slowed when they saw her stop, turning back to look. Lili shrieked once, then went silent. None of the others made a sound.

For a moment he only stared in silence, his boots making strange currents in the river of not-quite water flowing down the middle of the tunnel. Saya thought he might never make a sound at all, and they could simply continue on their way, but that little fantasia was quickly undone.

"Here!" he shouted. "Here they are! Here!"

Saya turned to Sotta. "Quiet him."

Sotta did as he was told. Without pause. Without question. He trusted her more than he felt afraid. He rendered a sphere around the Glasseye, creating a space where waves of sound did not move, turning his voice into silence.

The Glasseye could see the afterglow of what Sotta had just done, but the soldiers could not. Not even the Priests themselves could see afterglow with their own eyes. Saya decided in that instant that it was safer to risk having more afterglow in the tunnels if it meant they could take away the one way the Glasseye had to warn the other hunters—his voice.

The shadow was trapped in a cocoon of silence, unable even to hear himself. Yet all he needed to do was take a few steps forward or a few steps back and his voice would return. Sotta could not render across spaces any larger than that. And he could not render new ones fast enough to keep up with a man at the pace of a leisurely stroll.

Saya lay a hand on Mara's shoulder. "Mara. Darkness. Pure pitch."

Mara was crying. But she nodded. She rendered a cube of space where light could not pass through, set around the Glasseye. A blotch of utter darkness blinked into existence, with the Glasseye lost inside it. He could not even see his own crystal lens to look for their afterglow, for his eyes needed light to see what the lens showed. He stood within a void, sightless, soundless.

She heard his feet splashing through the fetid waters, coming toward her. He could still simply walk out of the darkness as easily as he could the sonic cocoon. And he was trying to do that very thing.

Saya begged Holy Juna for forgiveness for what she was about to do. She turned to Raba. "Raba, cube." She raised the shadow of her hand and pointed to the center of the tunnel, near the ground. "There."

Raba did not need to be told twice. He was the strongest little boy she knew. He rendered a cube, the kind she had seen him make many times before, the width of her arm, perfectly even on every side.

The Glasseye staggered out of the void, suddenly able to both speak and see. But no sooner did he see Saya, than he tripped over Raba's cube, His arms shot out ahead of him. The crystal lens flew through the air. He splashed down in stinking water, showering the walls, sending a tidal wave of filth lapping up the sides of the tunnel.

Saya ran toward him, reaching him just as he went down. She dropped onto his back, straddling his neck. He tried to push up, but the force of her weight falling upon him slammed his head down, cracking his nose against the tunnel floor under the water.

He bucked and kicked and flailed his legs, but she pressed down on his neck with her hips, taking fistfuls of his hair, desperate to keep his face beneath the shallow water. He waved both hands ineffectually, reaching backwards for her, his fingernails clawing long bloody tracks down her ankles.

She looked up and saw her children staring at her wide-eyed.

"Look away," she told them. "Look away now."

They looked away. The man struggled and splashed, but in the end, he struggled less and less, and then he stopped moving altogether, his last breath bubbling up out of the still water.

She did not let go until she was certain he was gone. She climbed to her feet and began walking once more. She said nothing to her students. For what was there to say after that?

She led them through the darkness, and out of a broken drain. They had to push through a mountain of debris to open it. It did not often rain in Kasaban, but when it did the streets became rushing rivers, carrying everything not anchored with it, depositing it all before drains like this. Saya tried to remember the last time it had rained and she could not.

Why could it not have rained today, Holy Juna? Why could it not have washed away the afterglow I left behind and allowed us to live in peace?

The drain opened onto an old dirt track beside the edge of the city.

"Where are we going, Sayani?" Tana asked.

"We are near the graveyard of the gods," she told the children. "I will take us to the temple of Holy Juna."

The crumbling gods in the pit offered them no solace and the sun gave no reprieve. The old men in the dry markets offered no water, and the poor masters offered no shade. They were alone on these streets, separate from everyone, forever other.

The temple was their only solace.

Saya went to the familiar door between two enormous pillars, the room of blue walls within, walking through that everlasting midnight garden, between the prayer benches, her feet leaving prints of blood and ash and filthy water all down the long golden rug.

The incense of rose did not calm her this time. She walked to the front, falling to her knees before the space where the idol of Holy Juna would have been before the Priests replaced it with their own. There she prayed to the memory of her god, to beg forgiveness and ask for deliverance.

The children collapsed onto the benches behind her. Exhausted. Defeated. Numb. Too tired to cry. The only energy remaining to them was to stare or to quietly shake. The sight of them in so much pain broke her in two.

"Please help us, Holy Juna," Saya whispered. "Show us the way."

Two temple-mistresses emerged. They brought water for the little ones, and wet cloths to wipe the soot and dust from their faces. They never asked who they were or what had happened. They never chastised them for the stains on the rug.

"Please tell me what to do," Saya whispered.

The Headmistress Praetorian knelt quietly beside her. "Do you seek guidance, daughter of Juna?" She was fair of skin and dark of hair, eyes ever downturned in honor of Juna, as if it was she who was begging Saya.

Saya used every ounce of strength not to break down in the arms of this woman. She wanted so badly for her responsibility to come to an end. She could not be the one alone any longer. She wanted something or someone to release the pressure inside her, to take the weight off her shoulders.

But she could not. The children had no one but her. She had to be this. She had to be a strong stone. She had to be a pillar of strength for them all to cling to. She could be nothing else. She could not be the one who broke down. She could not be the one who collapsed in tears. She could not be the one who desperately sank into the embrace of someone else and begged them to take over the strain for her. Kasaban offered no solace for those who broke. It did not pick up those who fell. It did not wipe away the tears of those who wept.

"We are hunted, Headmistress," Saya said. "We have lost our home. There is no place left safe for us. I...I do not know what to do."

"Holy Juna protects," the Headmistress said.

"Can we hide here?" Saya asked. "Just for a day, while we find a way to escape."

The Headmistress Praetorian looked her dead in the eyes. "I know what you have done. I know who you run from. I know what they are. I know what they see."

"Is there any way to hide from them?" Saya pleaded.

"If they have found any of what you have done, they can follow you."

"Can they find us even here?" Saya asked.

"If they have two samples of a surface that has been stained with your magick, they can follow you like a hound follows a scent. Even if you stopped using magick now, they would not need to keep finding more signs, because the ones you already left behind will tell them where you are now. The only way is to keep moving in secret until their samples fade."

"But for how long?"

"If they seal it under glass, they can track you with it for hours, or even days."

"Days?" Saya felt her heart sink into oblivion. She realized every render she or her students had made to help themselves get away, to let them survive just a little longer, had one and all been double-edged swords. Her renders at the school. Sotta, Mara, and Raba in the tunnels. Each helped them survive a few minutes longer, but each time it only reset the period of time they could be followed. "We cannot keep running for two days. We haven't the strength to make it another hour."

"Every moment you stop moving, they grow closer."

"Is there no way to escape them? None at all?"

The Headmistress Praetorian kept her eyes down. She leaned in close and kissed Saya on each cheek, on the forehead and on the lips. "They can only follow you to where your afterglow tells them you will be. The only way to escape them is to give yourself a head start. Stay away from the roads. The basin is flat and dry, the earth hard packed, leaving no more footprints than walking on stone. The white desert sands shift on the wind, hiding the steps of all daughters of Juna. As long as you can remain out of their sight, an hour ahead of them as you cross the desert shall be all the head start you require."

"How long must we stay ahead of them?"

"Within two days you shall be free of them."

Saya paled. "That long?"

"Two days to be absolutely sure. And you must none of you use magick during that time. Keep walking, even at night. Northeast lies a great lake, or you may choose to follow the gold star southwest to the saltwater seas. Do you know how to follow the signs of spineleaf groves to find water in the ground?"

Saya nodded. She paused, a sudden truth rolling over her, its terrible implications coiling like a serpent about her throat. "I am not the first to come to you asking this, am I?"

Her face softened, and she gave an earnestly sympathetic look. "You think we who live for Holy Juna do not see what goes on here in her city? We have eyes to see, and ears to hear. No, you are not the first one who has come asking these questions."

"What happened to the ones who came before?"

"Some became what they were meant to be."

"And the others?"

"They did not survive."

Saya turned to her, eyes stinging red, too dry to cry. "It has been so long since I prayed to Holy Juna the way I should. I can never spare but a moment. And now it is too late. That is why she has forsaken me."

"Why then did you come here?"

"Because I did not know where else to go."

The Headmistress Praetorian took her hands and held them between her own. "You pray to Holy Juna every hour of every day. Your devotion to your family is itself a prayer to Holy Juna. The work you do for this love, the work that only you can ever know the full breadth of, is itself the sacrament. Submission does not mean servitude; it means sacrifice for love. The love you give makes you every bit as much a priestess of the goddess as I."

Saya smiled. It felt so good to hear someone say it. For someone to finally see all she did, to understand, to acknowledge everything she had given. The wave of feeling washing over her was so unexpected she nearly collapsed.

"I do not want this to be the end," Saya said.

"Holy Juna does not sit upon her heels and kiss the hand of the oppressor. She is a fighter. One who fights not for power or conquest, but for hope and love. For family. To protect the ones who mean the most. To express love through strength, and to have strength powered by that love."

Saya's eyes were stinging, her face tight, lips quivering with dry sobs. "That is how I try to live. Every day."

"Holy Juna is strong. She saves her faithful. She turns herself into a light so bright it outshines the sun, leaving no shadows and turning her enemies to dust."

Saya nodded along with the words she knew so well. "Yes, yes." She was overcome. She was shaking. "I hope every day I can be as strong as she."

"Is that the Holy Juna you wish to be?"

Saya nodded emphatically. "Yes. I want to be her."

"What is your name, child?"

"Saya Ani Anai. Saya. The teacher."

"Well, Saya Ani Anai, you say you do not want this to be the end for you." She made a stern face, at last turning up her gaze, staring hard into her eyes, immobilizing her, pinning her in place and time, searching deep into the very soul of her.

"Yes," Saya said.

"Then make this not be the end."

Saya nodded. She rose to her feet, and turned, looking at her students. Such sweet children. It had always been her pride to help them learn. It was her joy to see them grow. She smiled at each of them, giving every one their moment to see her seeing them back. Knowing them. Loving them.

"Holy Juna is with me," she told them. "I do not want this to be the end. But if it is, it will be okay. Because we are together."

She heard muffled shouts from the streets outside. A door somewhere in the temple opened and swiftly closed. She heard a pair of slippered feet scrambling through the back corridors.

Another temple-mistress rounded the corner. She did not need to speak. Her face said it all—agonizingly sympathetic, on the verge of apologetic. She glanced over her shoulder back the way she had come, a gesture that told Saya her time had run out. There would be nowhere else to hide from the Priests. They were already here.

I'm not ready. It is too soon.

Two of the temple-mistresses barred the front door. A third began snuffing out the candles.

Sotta, Mara, and Raba stood as one, holding hands.

"Let us stay behind," Raba said.

"It is us they follow," Mara said.

Sotta nodded. "We used magick in the dark of the sewer. No one else. Without us for them to follow, you can go far. You can escape."

"You can be free," Mara said.

If she had not already been crying, those words would have wrung tears from her all on their own. Her wonderful little ones. How brave they were. Eight, ten, and twelve years old, and each stronger than any grown man or woman she had ever chanced across.

She knelt before them, wrapped an arm around Raba, and rested a hand on the shoulders of the other two. "No," she said. "No, I will not let you stay behind. None of the others will either. We all go or none of us do."

"Yes," Lili said. "We are one family. When many support each other, they can hold up long after they should have fallen. Sayani always says so."

The other students lined up behind her.

Saya looked at the three who offered to remain. "You heard them. Now what are we to do? Should we stay here and hide in the dark? Or stand tall in the light of day and fight for all to see?"

"For all to see," Raba said. He was trying so hard to be brave, but his lip trembled at the weight of his words.

Mara nodded. "For all to see."

"For all to see," Sotta agreed.

She looked at her students and beamed a proud smile at them each in turn. "What do I always say to you when I tuck you each into your beds at night?"

"We will go far away from here someday," Lili said.

"One of these tomorrows will lead us to a better life," Faloush said.

"As long as tomorrows keep coming," Aafi said.

"One of them will be that day," Sotta said.

"And the good thing about tomorrows," Mara said.

"Is that there always is one," Tana said.

"Whether we live or die, we are going someplace better than this," Saya said. "And it will all be okay. Because we will be together."

The Headmistress Praetorian pointed around a corner behind the shrine. "A door. To the street behind. It is the best chance you will have."

"Thank you," Saya said.

"Holy Juna would tell you to thank yourself. Now go."

Saya roused her students and ushered them down the corridor, following behind them, making sure none were ever lost to sight. Already she heard a pounding at the front door. Shouting. Heavy impacts shuddered the walls, cracking the wood.

By the time all the children were around the corner, she heard the door snap in two. As she passed through the veils behind the shrine, she glanced over her shoulder and saw a Priest in white storm into the room, gold mask silently screaming, hand shoving a temple-mistress out of his way.

Saya fled before she could see any more, but she heard the boots of soldiers, and the squeal of the benches being shoved across the stone floor. She prayed everyone who had helped her would be all right.

She finally turned another corner and saw a red door, bordered by a square of bright yellow light. It was a midday sun outside. It would be hot and blinding.

When the door opened it was like a wave of liquid bright splashing over her skin, smothering her eyes, searing her hair. The heat kicked each breath down her throat. Her sandals scraped across the sand, and the hot wind dried her hair to straw, and turned her skin to saltwater.

She raced down the avenue, jostling past people too proper to step aside and too startled to shout after her. Together they crashed into the middle of the street, running for dear life, forcing the wealthy aside, sending them stumbling into the high white mountains of dust the dunemakers had broomed to either side of it. Someone shouted after them. She felt someone dip into the source of magick behind her. The Priests were here.

Ahead she saw two soldiers, wrapped head to toe in ivory linen, hooded and gloved, even their spears wrapped in cloth to keep them becoming too hot to hold in the sun. Saya tethered a bubble of invisibility about herself, wide enough to cover the children as well if they did not stray too far.

Saya diverted them down another alley, threading the narrow space between the temple and the office of the mercantile registry. Their eyes could not see her, but the Glasseye lenses could. Their Glasseyes had tracked her and the children from the sewers to the temple in under an hour, using only their afterglow.

They were not chasing her, or her students. They were chasing the echo of what they had already done. They could read the light of the afterglow and follow it to the one who made it. There was no way to stop them. It would lead them to her and to her students no matter what. The afterglow was ruthless. It was relentless. It hated her for creating it. It would give her away to them at its first opportunity. It would tell them everything they needed to find her. There was no way to stop it.

Even if she remained invisible forever, their tools would tell them her precise location. She was only delaying the inevitable. The weight of that realization struck her when she emerged in front of the temple, beside the very doors they had just broken through to pursue her. A larger-than-life carving of Holy Juna marked the wall above her, reaching up as high as the temple roof.

At first no one came for her. A crowd gathered outside observed the temple doors, expecting someone to be dragged out through it in chains. Saya saw soldiers among them, and Priests. None acknowledged her.

She allowed herself, for just one moment, the thought that they might be able to get away, to run invisible through the deserts and the mountains until the magick faded. They could be free of the Priests forever. Free of eternal fear. Finally have a chance to be real people and not ghosts.

But that thought did not last.

She glanced over her shoulder, hoping her eyes would reveal a way out. But every doorway was blocked, every alley full, the streets in every direction choked with the street soldiers and holy guards, Glasseyes and Priests.

She rallied the little ones around her before the temple, Holy Juna hovering on the wall above, stoic face of weathered stone.

The hunters poured out of the alley behind her. They flooded out the temple door. Priests in deathly white, golden masks reflecting the sun in her face. Glassdogs in rough leather, eyes encased evermore in crystal goggles. Soldiers, hooded and masked, steel in their hands.

At the head of them was Sevastin Karda, the mark of the tear visible upon his mask, dripping from one infinite black eyehole. The White Death of Kasaban. *Burner of children.* He had been looking for her for a long time, and now he had come to claim his prize.

"I know you are there, Teacher," Karda said. "I know that you can hear me."

Saya bit her lip. She wanted to curse him and scream at him until her lungs bled. But that was what he wanted. For her to give him a sign where she was. He must have known his people were so close to triangulating her position. He was toying with her for the cruelty of it.

"I have longed for this moment," he went on. "Give yourself in surrender now, and I, the Most Holy Guardian General of the Sacred Light, will spare the little boys. I am the spirit behind this mission. I am its driving force. It is a sin to hide. Surrender to me before these many people, let them see the power flowing from *him* through me, and they shall see the benevolence of the Lord of Truth."

That stopped her. The subtle promise of life was so rare in this world that she entertained it. *I could save some of them at least. At least a few.*

But Raba told her not to. "I want to go with you," Raba whispered in her ear. "We all go together."

She wanted to hug him until her arms fell off.

But what else could they do? The Glasseyes rounded the corner, holding up their little vials, chasing their own hands, staring through their crystal lenses. Following the afterglow to her.

"You have corrupted these young children," he said, his voice a roaring echo from within the mask. "You prepared the way for them to become hosts to the demons of darkness. Surrender to me, or I shall make you watch the little abominations turn to ashes before your eyes. They will roast. Their skin will melt and run like oil. And you shall count every tear, listen to every scream. So close you can feel their breaths, but be unable to help." He let the horror of his words sink into her, all the way to her marrow. "Unless you surrender to me now."

Again she refused to speak, to give away her location.

Her disobedience enraged him. "You are an abomination. You must know you never had a chance to stop the return of the Lord of Truth. Even your grotesque, oily, black heart, must have felt the inevitability of his light."

I do not care about your Lord of Truth, she wanted to scream at him. But she kept silent.

Karda licked his lips. "Do you want to know what the child told me before I crushed his little organs one by one?"

Saya clenched her teeth. Her eyes slammed shut. Her hands balled into fists, fingernails biting her palms. *Say nothing. Do nothing. Do not let him win.*

Every Glasseye in the city moved in around her, closing a circle about her cocoon until they had her.

"You will know the righteous fire of excruciation," Sevastin Karda said. "You will know it better than any creature who has ever poisoned this air with their breath. I shall see to it. Your screams shall be remembered. I assure you of that."

Saya felt the jaws of fate closing around her throat, reducing all her possible futures to one—agony. She moved her eyes everywhere, hoping for a way out, a way to go on. But everywhere she looked was another bar in that iron fence standing between her and a future.

Saya knelt, wrapping her arms around the children, bringing them in close, an embrace of many arms.

I am sorry, Holy Juna. I tried so hard to stand in your light. I wanted to shine so bright. I wish I could have done better.

The hunters stared through their crystal lenses. The Priests raised their hands, plunging their minds into the source, reaching for the pieces of magick to bind into a whole of impossible possibility to render into reality.

She hoped they would kill the little ones quickly, to spare them from the fires. She could not bear the thought of them suffering the way she had seen so many of her kind suffer before.

She looked at the lenses, eyes staring through them all. The gold masks, sunshine glinting off every one, biting a little blazing arc out of her vision, swarming her eyes with light.

Light.

She remembered the stranger in the alley, using a bright light to hide afterglow from the Glasseyes. Glasseyes could see the afterglow of any magi, follow it, trace it. But to do that, they needed to see the afterglow. If they could not see their instruments, then it would not matter what the afterglow said.

She looked up at the noonday sun, standing directly above her, as bright as it could ever be. She thought of Holy Juna protecting her faithful, and remembered that she could not only bend light to hide in a pocket of invisibility, she could also reflect light perfectly. She had made flat mirrors so many times before. She had made invisible bubbles so many times before. But she had never crossed any of the streams of shape from one to the other.

If she could bind the streams to render a bubble shape of reflection, she could put the bright sun of Kasaban into everyone's eyes. She looked up at the high sun.

She would do what her goddess did.

I will turn myself into a light so bright.

Saya held her breath. She reached into the source and drew together the streams, bound them, and rendered a spherical mirror around herself, wide enough that the little ones were all within it. Karda and all his many hunters outside of it. She complimented it with numerous mirrors, angled every which way, reflecting the light in all directions.

They could not follow her trail if they were blind.

The world outside her bubble erupted in light. The sun, once safely above the world, was now duplicated on the ground, reflecting a light equal to it in brightness.

The Priests retreated, their golden masks turning away. The soldiers cried out, throwing their swords to the dirt and scratching at their eyes. The Glasseyes hurled their lenses to the ground, blinded, slapping palms against their eye sockets, desperate to plug them up to spare them from the deluge of light.

The people in the crowd disappeared. The light washed out every detail, painting over edges and shades and hues, taking every image and obliterating them in Saya's eyes.

We need a head start. Hours at least. And with her renders being static, massless, without any physical quality, she could pour her strength into streams of duration, setting them to last hours.

She still held her original invisible bubble around herself, tethered to her body, so that it would move when she did. She held all the children close. "Stay with me," she said. "Do not stray. Hold on to me. Hold on to each other. I am going to walk us away."

And she did, easing herself out of the mirrors. She walked slowly, carefully, taking each step with the premeditated attention of a sculptor selecting which bit of stone to chip away to carve a perfect statue.

"Shield your eyes," she told them. "Do not look back. The light will fill your eyes until you cannot see."

The little ones obeyed. They were all such good little fighters.

Saya peeked out through her fingers, watching where each foot would fall. Everyone she saw was holding their arms up, trying to hide their eyes from the onslaught of the light. Within the invisible cocoon, she might as well have not even existed at all.

The Priests would not realize until they passed through the membrane of her mirrors that she was no longer standing there. Every Glasseye and Glassdog in the city had been looking at her light. They would be seeing spots in their vision. If they tried to look through their lenses, they would not be able to read what their instruments told them. They could not follow her until their vision returned. It was the best head start she could manage. It would give her enough time to cross to the edge of the city and find a way to flee.

She hoped.

She led her tiny band of children through the streets. Her feet swam the mountains of white sand and dust the way the fish swam in the pond. She could not go home, and she could not go to the temple. So she went to the only other place she could think of where she would be safe—Terak's shop.

The outside was pale white stone, square windows facing the sun shuttered and covered with triple layers of canvas. Terak lived in a world of perpetual night within, his little lamp a hint of dusk where she could always only clearly see his hands working atop his table. He was the last familiar thing she had in Kasaban. She prayed he could help her.

She knocked upon his door out of habit. She always had. One, two, three. One, two, three. Always. She could have just gone in, like any other, but she liked to let him know it was her. If this was to be the very last time she did it, she would do it the right way.

She pulled the door open and peered into the darkness. The tiny bulb of light from his table lamp stood out in the darkness. The walls to either side were lined with mountainous shelves and tables, stacked high with wares, shrouded in shadow. She had never bothered to investigate any of them. They had always simply been the shadowed topography of his realm, bounding the familiar path to his table at the far end.

Saya let her students in and walked them to his table. None but Mara had ever been here before, and they drifted like clouds in the night sky, staring all about, captivated by his domain.

"Is this where we will be safe?" Lili asked.

"I hope so, little one," Saya said.

Terak continued working until they stood directly in front of him, crushing tiny fungi of unknown origin into powders with a mallet, scooping them into glass bottles with a batwing spoon. He gently lay the mallet down and folded his hands before his face, elbows propped on the table.

Saya's heart shuddered in her chest. She did not know how it still beat. There was a fire in her blood and it was the only thing keeping her moving. She had been running for so long that standing still, even for an instant, seemed an impossible feat.

"At last you bring," Terak said. He peered down his long nose at them. "Good little ones."

Saya barely heard his words. Her ears felt stuffed with wool, and she had not caught her breath once since the moment the wall came down at the school. "It is the last time."

He paused, puffing out his lips into a frown, frosted with silver stubble. "Sooner or later, Kasaban comes for all."

"Yes," she said. "I wish it was the first of many times. But everything is at an end."

He smiled gap-toothed at her. "End, begin. Is all same. Is all one thing."

"I did not know where else to turn," she said. "I would not have come to burden you if there was any other way."

"Burden," he said. "No burden. This day is always to come."

"I have little money," she said. "But I can pay for supplies."

"Pay," he waved a dismissive hand at her, as if insulted. "What is this pay? No pay."

She sighed unexpectedly, overcome with gratitude. "Thank you."

He reached back to a shelf behind him and plucked a brown glass bottle from a shelf. He held it out to her. "Take."

When she did not lift her hand to it fast enough, he shook it impatiently. "Take, take."

The moment her fingers touched glass she knew what it was. "Aafi's medicine." She hugged it to her heart like a long-lost heirloom. She looked up at him with the most thankful of tears. "You kept a spare bottle on hand."

He shrugged as if it was of no consequence. "From long ago I see this day to come."

"I do not know how to thank you." She raced around the table and embraced him, despite his protestations. She closed her eyes and felt his whiskers coarse against her cheek. "I am so very grateful."

"There is group moving on from Kasaban," Terak said.

"A group?"

"They come to me for map. Leaving today." He gestured at her little sock full of silver coins. "Better place to use this."

"Would they let us buy our way alongside them? Or would they report us to the Priests?"

He shrugged. "Northmen. Foreign. People from wide world move on fast from Kasaban. Always."

She tucked the bottle into a small leather bag he gave her, as the children picked up what they could to eat from what little dried foods he sold. "Thank you again, Terak. Your help has meant more to me than anything."

"You are good girl," he said. "Like your mother."

"My mother?"

"Too good for this place," he said. "Kasaban is for death. Life deserves paradise. Far from here."

Saya moved to the back door, waving the children to her, counting them, making sure they were all still there. "We must leave now, Terak. They could be coming. I do not want them to find us here. I am afraid they will hurt you."

"Bah," he brushed off her concerns.

She raised a hand in goodbye. "May you live in health until it snows in Kasaban."

He touched two fingers to his forehead and waved them at her. "Live such life that you need never come back to Kasaban."

"Thank you." She held all of the children close, her heart broken yet somehow still full.

She rested her hand on the door latch and closed her eyes. She had always been weighed down by the fear of being found out, of being caught. She had been governed so long by that fear, that her whole life had been forged by it. She hated the way it felt, but she at least knew what it was, what to expect, what needed to be done to keep that fear at bay.

But now, for the very first time in her life, she faced a new fear—the unknown in front of her. She would have to find a new way to live. She would have to learn a new way to survive. It would require strength to battle this unknown. And discipline.

I wish it did not have to happen this way.

But wishing won't turn sand into water.

She did not understand this fear. She did not know how to wrestle with it, how to bring it to heel, how to defeat it.

I do not know how to defeat it...yet.

She pressed down the latch. She opened the door.

That day we have always been waiting for is finally today.

This is the new day that will lead us to a better life.

Once more she stepped from darkness into the brightest light. Her family followed after her, watching each other's backs, helping each other the way she had always taught them to.

I will be the light to lead you all away from here.

No matter what happens, it will always be all right.

Because we will be together.

The door closed and she left the last little piece of her old life behind. Kasaban was her past. Her future was somewhere else. It might be a paradise, or it might be a dead sun bleaching her bones. But she would go into it free.

Epilogue

PURDIKAS WAITED UNTIL the other Priests were gone. He divested himself of his white frock, and his mask of gold, standing in plain linen robes, yellowed with age and worn by the summer heat of Kasaban. Their humble nature felt right to him, righteous and strong, though a bit tighter in the shoulders than they should have been.

He wandered the compound, following connecting tunnels from building to building, never once setting foot out in the sun. The air was still and hot. It devoured his strength, drying his body from the inside out.

He made his way to the holding cells in the center of the compound. Brother Agam was there, still wearing the white robes of crusade—the color of purity, to ward off the profanity of the savage, to hide the stain of the white dust of Kasaban's desert.

Agam looked up from the book before him, eyeing Purdikas with concern.

"Does it shock you so much to see me so?"

"It is...unexpected," Agam said. "I was concerned you had been censured."

He laughed. "Punish me by sending me away from here? No place could be harder on the soul than the one in which I now stand. Being in Kasaban is my punishment."

"We should serve with joy and pride at being chosen for this," Agam said. "Every abomination we burn is an exaltation of the Lord of Truth."

Purdikas sneered at him. "So said to us by brothers whose slippered feet have never left the comfort of their own cathedrals."

Agam did not argue. He returned to his reading.

"Karda lay the blame at my feet," Purdikas said.

Agam raised an eyebrow.

"I know you have heard it."

Agam folded the book closed in his lap. He looked up thoughtfully. "You planned the raid on the red brick compound. She escaped. These streets are supposed to be ours. And now everyone knows there is a Teacher of magi that the Ministry could not catch."

"Is that why they have set me to this duty? To watch over a compulsory probationer?"

"It is work that I am set to do, and often," Agam said. "I do not scoff at it."

"I do not mock the work, it is just that...it has been long since I have been set to something...menial."

"Work worth doing is its own reward."

Purdikas chewed his lip. "We should have taken her on the streets, alone, as I suggested, and come back for her students later. Karda's obsession with tormenting them through emotional cruelty was our undoing. There should be no emotion in what we do. We are instruments of the Lord of Truth. Those who use magick beneath us are objects. We must view them without judgement. The magi of this city are pieces of wood. We either build them into our house, or use them as kindling. We should not be playing mind games with logs in a woodpile. It is ludicrous."

Agam shrugged. "Yet you approved his operation that day."

"At Karda's insistence," Purdikas said. "They were supposed to be mere children. He swore to me the Teacher was barely out of adolescence, weak, of the third tier at most. Nothing suggested that we would meet such resistance."

"We stirred a hornets' nest," Agam said. "Now she is an inspiration to the magi, a legend. They say she walks our streets in secret, blessing the magi who hide and train under our noses. This place is turbulent enough without our authority being questioned. Doubts cast long shadows."

"Karda loses them with his theatrics, and then blames me to save face. This was his doing, not mine."

Agam chuckled. "I would not worry too much about Karda. He has his own problems now."

"Meaning?"

Agam sat forward abruptly. "Sevastin Karda swore to the Exarch that the Teacher would be dead. Burned away by the white light of the Lord of Truth. Instead, rumors are burning across the city that she is still here, watching over her faithful."

"This is worse than I ever could have imagined."

"The red brick compound is being treated like a shrine by the magi of Kasaban now. They sneak to it to whisper prayers to the Teacher for protection."

"Karda is disgraced. The Teacher is a legend. Still they lay the wreath of blame at my feet." Purdikas closed his eyes in frustration.

"Perhaps this is an opportunity," Agam suggested.

Purdikas raised an eyebrow. "Opportunity?"

"They have placed you into this duty," he said. "What better way to demonstrate your worth than by taking the reins of the reeducation of one they have deemed impossible to indoctrinate?" He paused for a moment. "Perhaps that is what they intended. Perhaps they provided you this opportunity precisely because they know your worth, but cannot absolve you and promote you to replace Karda without a reason to return your prestige."

Perhaps he was right. Compulsory probationers were never easy to manage. Reeducating them was difficult, especially when their indoctrination almost always came as the result of tragedy.

Perhaps that would be the way Purdikas could regain his standing among his peers. He would set himself to the task with alacrity. He would dedicate all his energy to this purpose, and he would succeed. He would give them results better than they would have ever anticipated.

"I will commit myself to this duty," Purdikas said. "I will serve the Lord of Truth wherever he sets a task for me."

Agam folded his hands in his lap. "Do not worry. You have not been censured. There is time for your reputation to recover. Opportunities for good works are abundant in a place such as this." His lip curled into a smile. "With Karda's reputation in shambles, nothing lies in your way other than yourself. You may end up with a path to the Exarchate over all of Mekrash Valley."

Purdikas smiled. *Finally.* "You are right. Leave me with him. I will heed your advice, Brother Agam."

Agam smiled and left quietly.

Purdikas walked to the cell, peering through the eyehole in the iron door. He saw solitary youth huddled in the corner, likely dizzy from the tinwood leaf tea. He had been well-fed and watered.

"You no longer have to be afraid," Purdikas told him. "It must have been such a hard life, scraping the crumbs from the tables of others. I wish you had come to us sooner."

The boy looked up, his mouth tight with anger.

Purdikas sighed sympathetically. "Never again will you feel that way. Never again will you have to scrape and crawl. You shall have the honor and power you deserve."

He looked down at the name they had scrawled on the wooden tag dangling on a wire from the door handle.

Noqer.

The only survivor from the raid on the red brick compound.

Their eyes met.

"Your new name is Nazariel. It is the name of the spirit god of redemption, prayed to in the faraway land of Tyrelon. The angels of all religions are the servants of the Lord of Truth, and so shall you be. Nazariel means *success against all odds.* You will wear this name well. You will become one of us and forget that you ever had a life so hard before."

THE

END

Appendix: Magick

MAGICK - the creation of any unnatural result in reality by drawing out (pulling) streams of altered reality (also referred to as streams of possibility) from the source of infinite possibility (the Slipstream). It is a means by which those who are born with such a skill may temporarily and locally rewrite the laws that govern reality itself, such as making physical shapes out of nothing, changing temperatures, altering the buoyancy of a ship, increasing pressure, changing the way light bends, altering the heat conductivity of metal, multiplying gravitation, swapping the inertia of two object, generating friction between objects that are not in contact, etc.

General Terminology:

AFTERGLOW - the residual patterns of colored particles that occur when any streams have been brought together into reality. The quantity, color, and brightness of the afterglow is determined by the types of renders created, their magnitude, and how much time has elapsed since the render was created.

They are most often invisible to the naked eye, but can sometimes be visible when fresh. All afterglow decays over time (both true visible afterglow, and that which can only be seen through a Jecker monocle) and eventually disappears completely.

BLUESHIFT - a tinge of blueness to the core color particles specific to any individual magus. Indicates the magus is moving closer to the location of the residuals.

DECAY TIME - the time required for different forms and magnitudes of afterglow to become completely dispersed. The decay time can be affected by how confined a space they reside in, the altitude, the temperature, the presence of wind or water, or the presence of certain forms of smoke.

GLASSDOG - men trained and dehumanized until they are little more than animals, forced by Priests of the Ministry to wear leather goggles with the crystal lenses that allow them to see the invisible afterglow (and any sensitized fluorescence) left by recent use of magick, a process which frequently results in them going mad.

INTERDICTION - the act of using Stoppers in close proximity to a magus in order to take advantage of precedence effect, so that the magus would be cut off from access to the streams of magick he employs to render into magick.

JECKER MONOCLE - an oval lens of ranum crystal, a mineral that is highly reactive to residual afterglow of magick. Attached to the primary lens are four filters: white, rose, green, and blue. Each filter is made of a different mineral, and can be slid into place over the primary lens. Each filter can be used individually, and the white, rose, and green can also be used in combination to expose different aspects of the afterglow.

MAGI - anyone with the ability to both pull streams and bind them to render magick into reality.

PRECEDENCE EFFECT - a phenomena of the Slipstream in which a specific stream specific to a particular magus cannot be used by more than one magus or Stopper within a certain proximity (or even used twice by the same magus at the same time).

REDSHIFT - a tinge of redness to the core color particles specific to any individual magus. Indicates when magi are moving farther away from the location of their afterglow.

RENDER - a separate a distinct magick result generated by the combination and binding of multiple streams. A unified fabric of possibility translated into reality.

RENDER TRACER - anyone trained in the arts of detecting, tracing, and apprehending rogue magi. Often armed with tools that are reactive to the presence of the afterglow of magick. Commonly and derisively referred to as Glasseyes.

SENSITIZED FLUORESCENCE - the attaching of afterglow to people, clothes, or other physical objects that it comes into contact with, resulting in stains that can be seen through a Jecker monocle. These decay over time just as the afterglow itself. The decay time of sensitized fluorescence can be affected by washing with water, the use of certain herbs, and the smoke of certain plants.

SLIPSTREAM - the source of all streams, the realm of pure possibility that any magi must reach into with their minds in order to create magick.

STOPPERS - those trained to reach their minds into the Slipstream and hold the streams of a particular magus in order to prevent that magus from employing them to create magick.

STREAMS - the building blocks of magick that magi must match together and combine in a specific fashion in order to achieve a coherent result. A different stream is required for each aspect of the desired result.

TINWOOD LEAF - a plant with sedative properties that make concentration extremely difficult, and as concentration is critical to the pulling and binding of streams, it can render magi inert for as long as it lasts, and can be administered indefinitely. It is the most common method of sedating magi.

THE FIRES - the general term used to refer to the most common method of ensuring magi ares destroyed.

From The Author

This has been one of the most rewarding journeys in my life. It has been my dream to write stories for as long as I can remember. It makes me truly happy to finally be able to share them with you. This has been my dream. Thank you for making it possible.

From the bottom of my heart, I want to say thank you for dedicating your time, and lending your imagination, to this story. The words I write are only one half of the bargain. Stories need readers in order to become what they were meant to be. You make them complete by welcoming them into your imagination. Thank you for joining me on this journey.

If you enjoyed your time with The Light Of Kasaban, please, consider rating and reviewing it on Amazon. It makes a world of difference. It is the single greatest way you can support authors and stories you love. And it is the best way to help your fellow readers know whether this journey is right for them. Your recommendation has the potential to help get this story into the hands of someone who truly needs to find it.

Writing is what drives me. It is my greatest passion. It is a challenge I look forward to every day. I hope to be able to keep doing it for all my days. I would love it if you could help make that dream come true.

I will never stop writing. I want to keep doing this until never meets forever. I hope to see you there. Until then, live for today, my friends. I'll keep dreaming, you keep reading.

Only always ever now.

Sincerely,
Thomas Howard Riley

Thomas Howard Riley currently resides in a secluded grotto in the wasteland metropolis, where he writes furiously day and night.

He sometimes appears on clear nights when the moon is gibbous, and he has often been seen in the presence of cats.

He looks forward to going further on this journey with you. He likes to reward those in his reader list with updates, lore, early access, and extra content.

Join in the fun by subscribing to the *luminous newsletter* over at:

THOMASHOWARDRILEY.COM